JOSEP LLOBERA CAI writer based in Edinbu *a duck* is the self-trans novel, which he wrote while studying Aerospace Engineering in Barcelona. The release of this self-translation is accompanied by the release of a new revised Spanish edition and it commemorates the seventh anniversary of its original publication. Apart from English and Spanish he also writes in Catalan and has a trilingual collection of poetry due for publication in 2022.

MARIAN F. MORATINOS is a Mallorcan artist based in London, one of the many cities which inspired her to create mixed-media artwork centred around scenes of the urban imaginary. Always in the search of new languages, her work blends design, illustration, printmaking and other visual forms. Marian has exhibited her work internationally in numerous exhibitions, art fairs and galleries and has worked on a wide range of projects for different clients and organisations.

NECESSITY IS A DUCK

Josep Llobera Capllonch

Original title: *La necesidad es un pato*
Copyright © Josep Llobera Capllonch, 2014

English translation © Josep Llobera Capllonch, 2021

Cover art © Marian F. Moratinos, 2021

ISBN 979-85-05171-77-6

Typeset by the author
Printed and bound by Kindle Direct Publishing

josepllobera@icloud.com

Self-translator's note

Dear reader,

During those long, sad, beautiful nights that I so warmly remember, when insomnia fell on me as both a curse and a blessing, I would write. Used to tell myself: 'these words will be my escape, these words will change my life'. What came out of them in 2014 is what I titled La necesidad es un pato, *a novel of introspection.*

The volume you are now holding in your hands, Necessity is a duck, *is the product of a prolonged process of self-translation. Klosty Beaujour described, in her book Alien Tongues, this process as 'the rite of passage, the traditional, heroic, physic journey into the depths of the self (a version of Freud's self-analysis or Joseph Campbell's archetypal voyage) that is a necessary prelude to true self-knowledge and its accompanying powers.' I wanted in this note to give credit to her words, for this is how it really felt. Thus, I do believe* Necessity is a duck *benefits from this increased awareness of the self as well as from an ex-*

tra layer of multilingualism. However, to call it a better, truer or even deeper version would be to undervalue the naivety and uncertain hope with which the Spanish original was written.

And like in every journey, the companions one meets along the way and without whom the hero would stand no chance: Huw Lewis, Francesca Hemery and Liam Hendry. I want to thank here in this note Huw for reading my last drafts of the translated novel and giving me his knowledgeable advice so generously. I want to thank Francesca for her friendship, the long hours in that coffee shop going through my early drafts and for the patience shown while arguing with stubborn me about language minutia. Last but not least, I want to thank Liam for encouraging the boldest of my translatorial decisions.

Now I'd better say no more.

Courage,

    Josep

Necessity is a duck

*To Núria, and to the memory
of Hermann Hesse*

There is no greater beauty than recognising, in the greys and greens of reality, the iridescent shapes of dreaming. Then it is as though we had dreamed them twice.

First Part

I

Why is it your discourse never changes, if every new time I address you I'm a different person? Don't you hear my voice deepening? Or maybe what you want is for me to bear your cross? I don't remember having signed any agreement, you are in no manner beholden to me, neither am I beholden to you. I don't wish you any harm but, how do you expect me to wish you well? How do you expect your tired words to sound beautiful and wise to me? How, if every one of them belittles the words of the poet who is nothing but heart?

II

It was quarter to seven in the evening, the light was weak but bright enough to let me see the cloudy sky and its sad grey colour. It wasn't raining but the air was thick and the atmosphere, tiresome.

I went to class despite knowing what awaited me there, but it was already a boring day, so I really didn't care. However, the teacher began his talk and a minute later I was already regretting taking shelter from the dark evening outside, within that classroom whose walls were rocking me like a cradle would. Little by little the silence was muffling the explanation, an endless lullaby. My eyelids weighed two, three, four hundred tonnes, their mass ever increasing the more I resisted. And there I was, in a seemingly tempting position, alone in the very last row. But whoever was present would know I was going through martyrdom, as there were only fifteen seats, seven occupied, eight empty. So neither his myopia nor the thickness of his contact lenses mattered, nor did the veracity of my pretence, the nobleness of my motives nor the meanness of his: my eyelids, my guillotine.

Everything, absolutely everything has its moment. Even happiness itself, when inopportune, can become barbed wire. Like the cradle of red-hot bars, sharp spikes and cutting springs. Like the lullaby that scourges me, every lash with more anger and less shame!

And I bend my knee, I, ignorant sinner. But I raise myself alive, wiser with every step! For it is in sin, my friend, where pardon lies, where remorse succumbs and finally dies. Where love is born, and prospers…

I had, for five minutes or so, escaped. I had, away from the obtuse walls of reality, discerned a clairvoyant unconsciousness. I felt virtuoso, inspired, relaxed. But the teacher, bad-tempered, pissed off by my overdrooling mouth resting pleasantly upon my desk, grabbed the nearest piece of chalk and hurled it at me while in my mind were sliding what I humbly believed were words of wisdom. Everybody pulls the same stupid face before naked knowledge. But I, having had a rude awakening, then I was irate, furious, insanely mad. Blood was boiling in my head, its reddish steam bursting out of my nose and ears like a fighting bull. Like a derailed train! I strongly snatched the desk up and mindlessly threw it at his gargoyle head with the brute strength of an animal.

Seen as a cold act from the outside, those fearful eyes described it to me as almost cruel. They were astounded, dumfounded, bewildered, in shock, a bouquet of smartarses who had just stopped taking notes for the first time in three years. Had that altercation been covered in the final exams of next week, the class might have been able to describe the facts, but unable to extract any moral, to find the cause nor to intuit, even, a further consequence than my mere expulsion from university. They were condemned to learn chalk on slate.

Though I still consider my action was one of madness, I decided at the time to attribute it to a deliberate consciousness, for I had never felt any better and, were I to take any credit for that, it just wouldn't be in the capacity of a madman. Then, in the quietest silence, feigning a sense of ease with a half-smile and a confident pace, I walked out. Maybe not completely different, but certainly somewhat changed.

III

The thick clouds had disappeared; I was walking with my mind dazed, blank. And I kept on going this way, it seems, a long while, for when I went to ask myself where should I go and what should I do, my steps, always ahead of me, had already taken me to the beach. I sat down, with my bare feet buried in the sand.

In the sky the moon was reigning.

If I had to choose an adjective to define that night I would decide on 'clear'. At least this was how I saw it, there was still some cloud but the enormous moon of the summer solstice had swept away all the stars from the sky, this was her night and I couldn't take my eyes off her.

The hours went by as if waves breaking the shore. One wave, two waves, three waves, four o'clock... Morning was approaching and I was still awake, trying to imagine the dreams of those who were already asleep. In our dreams we often come across people of unknown faces and motley characters, but there also appear people we do recognise; whether they be our closest core of family and friends or that much wider periphery of acquaintances barely known and strangers barely spotted: the nameless baker, the brisk waiter who's always telling the same jokes, the girl that looked at you on the train, the weird guy who sat next to you and smelt so bad… Would I appear in any of their dreams? But at that moment my mind drifted elsewhere… a memory of my first university year which up until that day I had overlooked. I know it was not a dream, but when recalling it I perceived it as such.

I see myself talking with a person I recognise in a place that is not even physical, I don't remember how I arrived there nor why I was talking to him and, nevertheless, I find sense, listen, reply and even ask questions and make friendly jokes. Phrases fly from one's mouth to the other's ear but I don't pay much attention to the banal exchange of word; rather I prefer to remain absorbed in my thoughts as I don't really care about his. Suddenly, I become aware of my surroundings, trees materialise, a car park and a river of students arguing about maths problems and exam scores; I hear birds chirping over the hum of traffic, a bicycle's *ring-ring*… but my interlocutor's proposal muffles it all at once, and as the stars were swept away by a greater light earlier that same night so does the dreamlike image is swept by the echo of our lasts words:

'Don't think twice, just come.'

'I'm sorry, I can't.'

'I'm offering you happiness. Don't you want to be happy?'

'Of course I do but I can't, I have an exam on Monday and have to study. I'm sorry.'

And this is how my memory-dream ends, with me refusing happiness. I think that he was inviting me to a party. Nowadays I don't enjoy them much (to feel forced to drink by peer pressure, see myself surrounded by people who want to make a spectacle of themselves pretending to be something or the other, to smile when not feeling like it…), but at that time, before getting used to Loneliness, way long before falling in love with her, I loved company and mundane life.

It could be that the renouncement of this ephemeral and hollow happiness was, without my knowing it, the start of my pilgrimage to something deeper and long-lasting. It's true that I hadn't taken any step yet, but it is with the idea of departing that every journey does start. It could be that, not having paid the proper attention to it, that conversation had been eating away at me over the years. Through books I didn't dare to read in the past, through real characters of strange tastes whom treat I used to repudiate, through songs I previously refused to listen to; even in my sleep it was whispered, rumbling in my dreams. The message was always there, between the lines, hidden for me to find, telling me that there were other things to worship, and without having to exhaustingly carrying out sacrifices in vain! That I had to satisfy my wishes never fearing their nature and, in the worst case scenario, if having none, then go and seek them.

After declining that invitation the parties I went to were no longer the same, free will didn't reign in them anymore but protocols, appearance and farce. But that's life, fictitious beyond belief, and it is on us to make it real, interfering with it; to poke it with a stick to see how it reacts. Or with a classroom-desk!

That was exactly what I had done that autumnal summer evening after three years of university. Half-conscious of my submission, I finally rebelled against everything previously learnt and lived. And at that moment I found myself as though I had just woken up, opened my eyes. As though, being in automatic mode, I had not taken any decision in my life, as though more than living it I had been just observing it all these years.

I had always considered myself intelligent but, what is intelligence?, who is intelligent and who is not? Is it perhaps he who decides to be a blameless citizen or he who doesn't want to be another brick in the wall? The one who imposes his own law or the one who adapts? Who amasses knowledge in solitude or who is always surrounded by people that love him? The nutty scientist or the international athlete? The actor or the spectator who observes in silence? He who raises a family or he who gives it up? Who achieves success or the unrecognised artist? Who longs for freedom or who dreams to build his empire? Who broods over everything or who can sleep at night? The poet or the lover? The sane or the mad?

Then I was questioning everything! Why did it take me so long?

I suppose that's because as kids we are educated to do whatever comes along: we mingle with the closest, listen to our parents, do our everyday duties, study, play football, eat whatever they serve us, watch the shows and films that are on TV, we sleep at night and are awake during the day, have lunch at one o'clock and have dinner at half seven…

Christmas, red and white, always falls within the same exact dates.
It's never different, it's always December in December.
As August, the eighth, is sizzling and warm,
it always brings us a new year
January the cold month.
And it commences again,
the cycle will cycle unchanged,
like it did before and it will do ever after.
People don't change, as neither does their foolishness,
they suffer death as they celebrate when born that someday will die.

But when do we decide? Why can't we choose that which is not offered to us? Is it because we are incapable of seeing the alternatives?

How had I reached this point? Why did I not appreciate my current situation when others would have killed to be in my place? However, horror doesn't appear when realising we are someplace we don't want to be, but when with our eyes closed, trying to envisage some alternative to our imposed destiny, we see nothing, only darkness, lights off, those of the imagination, those of desire.

Then, why should that night seem to me so clear? Everything felt strange and confusing. Nothing I had fought for was left standing; everything had caved in, been ripped to shreds, and no matter how much I wanted to assemble the pieces together these didn't fit together anymore. Maybe they never had. But it wasn't until that night, in which I measured time in waves, that I eventually became aware of it.

As the morning was getting closer the pieces kept cracking and bursting and when the sun emerged from the surface of the sea, huge and red, what had been my life was no more than dust. And it was the breeze that spread it all along the beach, among sand, shells and salty water, as if the ashes of a corpse. Because if when at sunset I found myself a stranger, when dawn broke I had already died and been reborn.

And hence the night was clear, its lull allowed me to comprehend my confusion was that of a newborn; and that's why, even though I had never been this lost, I knew exactly what to do: begin again!

IV

And in the manner a newborn knows about the breathing trick and where the milk is kept… how naturally he closes his lips round the nipple and sucks it up… In the same manner knew I that I had to go to the bank, withdraw all the money from my savings account and, thereupon, set off for the airport. Luckily that year I had been granted a decent scholarship so I could afford any destination. When I arrived at the airport I had the afterthought it might have been a good idea to stop by my student accommodation to fetch some clothes, have a shower… but this thought lasted only a few seconds, since I was actually carrying with me everything I wanted and needed: my brown leather jacket, my favourite t-shirt and the bag with my black notebook… where would I go without my black notebook?

It might be the fact of having no idea of which heading to take, or the haunting remnants of my prior sorry self, but the truth is the first destination that came to my mind was Mallorca, which for eighteen years had been my home and where my family still lived. I believe it was more due to the latter. I couldn't leave without saying goodbye, without giving them any explanation. And that meant two things: that part of me was still rather alive and I had, precisely for that, to go there so I could finally get rid of it and start being myself.

And so I did, even knowing that just as I stepped in it would come tumbling down, going home was the only option that my conscience would allow itself. I was going to set forth on what I sensed was going to be a grandiose voyage, leaving everything behind, thus my must was to bid farewell to those people who had raised me and loved me so much. Perhaps they were the reason why it took me so long to awake and see life free from schemas, to understand, to understand per se. When we are loved we suffer a severe comfort that numbs us. That comfort is very restful but we shouldn't mistake it for happiness, for they are not the same thing. Happiness requires nerve, curiosity about oneself and to be willing, above all, to get up from the sofa. But it's not just that. How are you to abandon those who have literally given everything for you? It's hard to say goodbye to family and friends, and nevertheless people do it constantly: they go to study far from the nest —like I did— or they move abroad searching for a job, they get married… And still they keep in touch, they exchange correspondence, they use the phone and get to visit each other every now and then. But mine was a different case; I wanted to go never to return, to fade in my going like a light blown away. This was what I wanted to do, what I needed to do. But I was feeling as if I were betraying those who I owed my life, and that was killing me.

I had shed tears in solitude so I could keep calm when the moment came, so they would notice the tingling in my stomach and not, the trembling of my bones; so they would hear in my voice the serenity of a man and not, the babbling of a child; so they could see, among its enclosing darkness, the reflection of that little flame in my living and tearless gaze…

Well, that moment had come. I inhale, exhale, the truth shall be told. I opened the door and went stealthily in. She didn't turn around, kept cooking unaware of her unexpected guest. But I didn't approach her, I remained quiet behind, leaning against the kitchen wall and watching her cooking. I had always enjoyed seeing her this way, taking her time so her loved ones could devour in minutes the fruit of her hours. And I admired her for her altruism and her almost incomprehensible love. But at that precise moment she was acting in haste and even looked slightly wrinkled, consumed by the years gone by that had agreed not to reward her devoted generosity.

The shattering noise of a dish dropped on the floor disrupted my divagations to bring me back into a household whose matriarch had just frozen up. I said 'hello', and she, despite us being separated just by two metres, ran to me and hugged me tight. Then, her joyous face of joy clouded my brain, my eyes, and made reason, mine and the world's, fly through the air; silencing thus my so rehearsed speech. The truth shall be told but it would break along with the dawn next morning. That night, however, I would make a truce with myself to believe whatever my eyes might see and whatever my ears might hear, even if what I heard were my deceitful words and what I were to see, their false consequence.

Time would slow down while mother passes the breadbasket over to me, and father ends telling one of his jokes with an endless guffaw, one of those laughters that are easily spread among commensals despite arising from the silliest joke. Then, we all start laughing and laughing while the meal gets tepid then cold, but we are all together again and to mitigate our hunger is the least of our worries at this round table, which is not formed by knights but indeed by great people, people who even though knew me well, and knew I was not, kept treating me as if I were a God.

It happened just like that. And like a despicable being, late at night, I disposed myself to tell the truth with no louder noise than the gliding of my fountain pen and the folding of a sheet of paper. However, when facing the blank page, I realised it was impossible for me to explain it all. I wasn't understanding anything, at that moment I was pure heart and intuition, I was unable to express what neither of these two had to say but I could feel them, and, although that could be too little for the others, it was more than enough for me. But that letter was indeed for them and maybe that was what was stopping me, the incessant hunt for their approval. I had never felt a slave and, nevertheless, I was one.

I closed my eyes; silence; darkness, that of the night; light, that of the moon; alone before the border that separates the world from nothingness, searching for the words that would allow me to cross it and meet the path I was so anxiously yearning to walk. I knew it, I knew the memories would torture me with as much determination as they had cheered me up in the past, but to confront reality was the best chance I stood to flee its realm. As surely as fire burns wood I knew it and another log would soon roll onto the hearth.

When I reopened my eyes and saw the page blank, the border had already dissipated and blankness become inviting. I could write with total freedom, with no restrictions nor fears, since for its thunderous reading I would already be far away; a little closer to me, or perhaps even further from everything I had ever been.

At that moment I felt as if I were the writer beginning to narrate what were going to be my adventures, and the sheet was totally blank, I could write whatever I wanted, be whatever I wanted. And possessed by this so intoxicating yearning I wrote a letter in one go, a letter with my own recognizable sinuous handwriting and words though with a soul I could not quite pinpoint within me.

Dear family,

I'm sorry for communicating with you through a letter, mainly because of the importance of the words I have to tell you. But these have been the most difficult I've ever written and can't begin to imagine how hard it would have been to speak them aloud.

Now you see this is not any greetings card nor any other sort of declaration of fondness, although I would like you to consider my mere desire to say goodbye as if it were one. Anyway, I advise you to take a seat to read the rest.

Here's the bombshell: I'm not going to sit my final exams. I have decided to abandon my studies. But it's not only that, I'm abandoning you and my supposed home as well. The reason? I guess that's because all these years I felt nullified in the university when, despite my apathy, kept moving forward along the path of the blameless citizen. I don't know, I studied, I ate, went out for runs and rested. This was my day-to-day life and I found it insipid to a great extent. But a series of experiences and reflexions led me to believe that this lack of motivation was the complement of an undesirable obligation and not an entity of itself; that we don't have to do over and over that which we hate until we perish old and bitter or, even more tragically so, young and hanged. I started to think that life could not only encompass survival, there had to be in addition a little magic, something that would make me wake up with illusion in the mornings and that would steal my sleepiness at nights, yet not as my worries and dilemmas do now but how would do so the clickety-clack of an eager mind.

And afterwards there came more thoughts, each thought darker than the former, until I got scared by my own madness and tried to make them stop. I tried with all my strength for weeks, even months, but who in his right mind would abdicate from thinking just out of fear of his own conscience? Nobody who appreciates himself. Even then I'm ashamed to say I have restrained my acts up till today, either for fear or loyalty to you, but it's been a long time that I've been carrying with me this smothering scream, which I, exhausted, can no longer contain. And that's why I'm screaming now, not because I'm angry with you or want to hurt you, but because I need to breathe.

I would like to be clear and concise, to tell you all this has a proper explanation, but it's getting impossible for me to describe further with words what propels me to the distance. Now I comprehend the world is as huge and minute, as simple and complex, as magical and obscure as we would like to see it. Then, why should I walk if what I really feel like is to fly?

This letter is to be read just once, don't exert yourself rereading it as you won't find any reference of my yet unknown destination, to disappear is my intention. But this doesn't mean I don't love you; what's more, tonight I have loved you more than ever. I just simply want to start a new life and I don't believe this would be possible without renouncing everything that I've been and I've loved.

I know I can't really ask you to understand me or not to judge me with severity, but I believe I can ask you to take into account that at the present moment I think and feel more than what I'm able to express.

And there I stopped, unable to sincerely write down my name. And although it said it was only to be read once I reread it countless times. How could that be possible? There materialised before me, in a snaky writing, words that expressed my frustration and will better than my comprehension would have ever allowed me to do. More than a creator I had acted as the receiver of those words and I didn't know where nor what was their transmitter. Maybe it was gestating inside me, maybe it was a god sitting on some sphere above, a writer perhaps. Maybe it was all those at once. Would that mean I was trapped in a book that I myself was writing?

Darkness began to retreat and with it, my divagations. I folded the letter and left it above the untouched bed. I decided to leave my bag and took only my black notebook and my leather jacket with me. I opened the door…

'Are you going for a run?' Asked my mother from the bed with her eyes still closed.

'Yeah, today I've woken up with the feeling of being immortal. I might even reach America!'

'In that case take the swimsuit too, the trainers won't work to cross the Atlantic,' said my father, whom my footsteps had also woken up, drowsy yet with sense of humour.

'Don't worry, more than immortal I feel like a winged god. I will cross it flying if I need to,' I like it when truth itself sounds like sarcasm, one can be honest, take a load off one's mind, and still lead the unaware interlocutor to believe it's all a simple joke.

… and left.

V

The doors opened and I walked into the airport. I breathed in the international air and sensed a familiar, yet strange sensation. It was as though, not having slept the night before, I had just worked out the last numbers of a final test. Those who have ever been in a similar situation will be acquainted with the state of euphoria I'm talking about: that exhilarating feeling of being capable of everything, either to write an epic poem or to run around the whole world. But we either go around the world so fast we don't even notice the changing landscape or that state is as powerful as it is fleeting, because the truth is one suddenly feels as exhausted as he who has fought with tigers and danced with dolphins; shattered, fit for nothing, just sleep. But as I said, it was a sensation somewhat strange: instead of saying 'that's me being freed', and rejoicing, I felt as if I had just vented my nerves and it was time already to go back home; like a bird in a cage that has forgotten how blue is the sky and what it's like to fly freely.

And now I was that bird who I before wanted to free; but not just any bird, I was a hawk. I didn't know whose hand opened the little cage and, at the same time, I curiously recognised it. A little squeak and there we were, lord and serf, in that part of the woods where little squawks go to die. Trees spring up, rivulets sprout from the ground, pebbles pile up and, right beside, on top of a pronounced rock, there appears a desk upon which the literature teacher is leaning. She was just as I remembered, with her ginger hair, her thick-rimmed glasses, that same black, short and tight skirt, her thin legs covered with dark and delicate silk, and her white half-open blouse… What a blouse! She was now holding a book and reciting verses I couldn't hear. I thought I was going deaf. Then, a sudden rustle of dry leaves comes to my ears, something monstrous is approaching. Huge, fast and heavy are its strides, so bold and self-assured as not to bother about how loud they are. Abruptly, the ground stops trembling and, frightened by the unmistakable silence that precedes any carnage, I take off, gaining speed as I gain altitude. When I'm flying by the teacher, however, I slow down trying to catch a glimpse of her breasts which she has just covered up with the book she's holding, is that my name on it? She slides her hand under her skirt… I'm so aroused! Then I want to stop, but I can't manage to control that alien body that forces me to keep ascending. And now it's night already, wolves pay tribute to the immense moon with their sad and beautiful howls. Magic is all around, but horror does not cease, the moon becomes sun and here soars a blaze, here are my wings melting! I wake up fluttering, but if before I was a hawk now I'm a duck… A sharp knife unsheathed, my body lying on the floor, now bird now human, a rapturous face, an isolated moan of pleasure…

'Are you ok?'

How much I would have loved to say that I had never ever felt any better, to kiss her on her lips and get up with a somersault! That girl was the most beautiful thing I had ever seen. However, her presence had a rather anaesthetic effect on me, for when I raised my hand to check if her reddish hair was indeed scorching, I fell unconscious once again; but in her arms this time, those of an angel.

When I came back to my senses it was she who was caressing my hair. The tiled floor had been replaced by a bench, my head fallen onto her thighs. I have always liked the films made in Hollywood, their actors always uttering the most opportune words. However, that scene demanded silence, Clint Eastwood knew that, and so did I: my newly-opened eyes mirrored in hers, mirrored in mine… we were strangers, globetrotters catching our breath at the airport, listening to the travellers' steps as the sailor listens to the waves before setting sail.

Later on I would write about that magical instant in my notebook:

Our world is not such an inhospitable place after all: there are fruits hanging on the trees; in the rivers, fresh water meanders; birds in the air, fishes in the sea; in the woods, hares, wild boars and little lambs. But such a calm… such a calm can only be found in those oases whose coordinates don't belong to any physical place but which are lost amid soul and happenstance. Hence, the desert world we see; we are being dragged to death by the sands of time.

We remained in silence I don't know for how long, an instant perhaps, perhaps a little longer, something out of proportion before our long and arid journey. But even though the goal of my departure was to lay down in a haven of peace like the one I had just found, I raised my upper body and sat up straight, placed my hand on her rosy cheek… Warm and slow seconds were those before my hand, obeying hers, moved from her rosy cheek onto her pounding chest. Through her dark wild eyes thousands of horses were galloping towards mine. I would have loved to kiss her, but there was something stopping me, later on I would know why. She flashed me a smile, mischievous rather than shy, and, not saying a thing, she turned around to grab her beige leather rucksack which she gracefully put on her shoulders as she stood up. She didn't look at me again, she simply walked off and left me there sitting alone. I wanted to go after her, but found my legs benumbed. I tried to shout then, but found my voice gone. Impotence was all I could feel as she was walking away. Where would she go? I could not see, she was walking towards a dazzling light growing brighter and, when she was barely a shadow, I stopped fighting against a body which would simply not move. And as soon as I stopped struggling and calmed down, the light grew dim enough to let me see the outline of her figure. She kept on walking but I did not mind any longer; with every step our mystery was taking shape and with every step it was easier to imagine a future encounter. I knew it, I knew it with all the assurance a cinema spectator might have when sees the soon-to-be-lovers bumping into each other, sharing a frame for the first time, and expects that, sooner or later, chance will bring them together once more. But where would she go? I could not see, she was walking towards a dazzling light growing brighter, she was barely a shadow…

All the leaves are brown… I listened and watched the light gobbling her down… *and the sky is grey…* Where would she go? *…I've been for a walk on a winter's day…* I could not see it, *…I'd be safe and warm if I was in L.A….* the light was growing brighter …*California dreaming on such a winter's day…* she was barely a shadow…

CALIFORNIA DREAMING! Fuck, another dream…

I recognised it immediately; I heard it for the first time in a famous TV series that narrated the life of Hank Moody, a successful writer, hopeless romantic and incurable womaniser with a gift for trouble and who lived, of course, in sunny California. I would always recommend it fervently when talking about cinema and series and commend its soundtrack. Then I didn't know if that particular song was part of the dream itself from the very beginning or if it had sneaked in from the outside, perhaps through the loudish mp3 player of a teenager or the humming of a redhead girl —me and my obsessions—. I opened my eyes, I was lying on a bench, much more worn-out than the one from my fantasy. I looked around in case there was somebody with headphones on and, effectively, there was a specimen sitting right next to where my head was resting. It took me some time to react and I kept staring upwards to its body odour, its grassy hair and hairy nostrils. It was far from the image of the silent girl. It, he or she, I don't know, I couldn't tell neither by its face nor by its way of dressing, it was one of those strange beings you find when leaving home and which makes you ask yourself where did it come from. Its face was a sort of a huge spot. I took my eyes off its face and focused on the song that was still playing.

The song was right, today was a winter's day, it wasn't sad but it was indeed melancholic: the clear sky looked grey, the warm air felt cold, thoughts were loud, and one could be easily fooled to hearing, even in the well-trodden airport of Palma de Mallorca, maroon leaves rustling under one's gait.

And the heart, yes, the heart!, let's call it by its name, was pushing me towards the warm west coast of The United States, the land of opportunity. Would it still be so on my arrival?

The song stopped playing, but I didn't need to listen anymore, I knew exactly where I had to go. I stood up and went humming to the first counter I found.

'How can I help you, sir?'

'A ticket to Los Angeles, please.'

I didn't expect that, I didn't count on it, I actually didn't want to fall in love, and even then I did.

VI

At some thirty-three thousand feet above sea level and at a 0.83 Mach speed, seated next to the window, as it should be, I was on my way to California without the idea of finding solid ground but with the hope of landing on the California I had dreamed of: silent, of reddish hair and wild gaze. My budget was generous yet not unlimited, so I saw myself forced to buy the cheapest flight the attendant girl could offer me. She wasn't too pretty, I thought to myself, while she was typing and looking at the screen; although, to be fair, I didn't think it would be possible, after that lively dream, to ever meet any other girl or woman that could impress me with her prettiness. Nevertheless she turned out to be very helpful, she took her time to search for the best deals on her computer and eventually came up with a very cheap combination of flights. The only inconvenience, she said, was that I had to stop over in London where I would have to wait the whole weekend for my final flight.

Inconvenience? This was how she sold it to me and this was what I got to believe. I even remained annoyed for about five minutes for having to wait that long, but my good mood, my hopes and will to comprehend made me embrace the so-called inconvenience as an opportunity to discover the real London. I had already been in the city before, travelling with my family, but we spent the whole trip doing exclusively that which is expected from tourists: we took a ride on the London Eye, went to Madame Tussauds Museum, a boat trip through the Thames, another ride in one of those red buses for tourists —if you take a look on your right you will see blablabla—, shopping at Harrods… We also went to a tea house where we asked for tea and shortbread, but we are Spanish, more of a *café con leche* sort of people, we laughed when seeing our faces puzzled by that foreign bitter taste which we were not used to, so we finished the shortbreads but we only drank two sips of that concoction and… We took photos!, piles and piles of photos, with Big Ben in the background, in the hotel clowning around and in the Natural History Museum… How much I liked dinosaurs in those days! But what I liked the most was to clown around, that was the funniest bit of being a tourist, one can afford to do all the silliness one is capable of and then giggle, titter and cackle. I still cannot contain a guffaw when recalling the face of that waiter after my father asked him for —literally!— "calamari fritti *a la romana*", or when my mother was making an excruciating effort to tell the chambermaid, with signs and exaggerated gesticulation, that the heating wasn't working; poor girl, how she blushed when she saw my mother blowing with all her might while wrapping up and down her arms around her body... What a picture!

There I was, at some thirty-three thousand feet above sea level and at a 0.83 Mach speed, seated next to the window, as it should be, flying over the vastness of the ocean but not the ocean itself, for although we were going fast and the clock was still ignoring my pleas for it to stop, when I looked through the window I didn't see that dense blue of paralysed waves but a projection of snapshots, some correlative and ordered, others rather dispersed and ill-piled up. As if the fact that I had left had altered the space-time equilibrium making, thus, all my possible lives in the island befall at once before my eyes. And there were some happy lives there but which were lived, nonetheless, like I had done so up till then, like I had glimpsed them at that very moment, as a spectator.

We did not take a long time to fly over the French coast, after all that was the Mediterranean Sea, neither ocean nor immense. There were still three hours of flight to go. I was still touched and excited but I could feel the fatigue spreading all over my body. My head was overheating, my eyelids were getting heavier with every second, my muscles were still in tension but I could feel them relaxing while admiring France from my privileged position. The continent was becoming blurrier also with every second, until I could only see the clouds that were covering it. The tension amassed in my body and mind vanished, I could do nothing but to relent and turn myself in to the latent darkness of my eyelids…

This time I had not been a victim of any illusion of my subconscious, rather it had been a restful sleep and so deep that the air hostess had to come expressly to wake me up. The Boeing was deserted, this had been its last flight for the day so I got to leave the plane together with the pilots and the hostesses like one more of the crew. The plane was connected to the terminal by a jet bridge, which obliged me —this kid that could wait no more— to bear Heathrow's Customs and its crowds before I could breathe the spring-like air that England had to offer.

The most sensible thing would have been to take the bus, to save money and stuff, but I could not help myself; when I spotted a row of traditional black cabs parked outside I had to take one.

'Where are you going, sir?' He asked with elegance and discretion, looking at me through the driving mirror. I had definitely made the right decision when taking that cab.

'To California,' I said in a totally determined tone, testing him.

'Excuse me, sir, I don't really know the address, is that a pub or a modish restaurant?'

Surely what first came to his mind was the sunny west coast of The United States; however, the taxi driver demonstrated exemplary manners when refusing to joke, and proceeded with the smartness of a limousine chauffeur. I stopped speaking with double meanings, he seemed to be an upright and firm man, he would keep ignoring my hints to establish a conversation with a more ambitious goal than the one of making my destination clear.

'Drive me to London, to the city centre,' I said, surrendered in the backseat, hoping to hear no more from his voice except for the journey's fare at the end of it.

I was surprised when I heard my tone, I had always felt alone but I had never been so really. I believe that was the reason I felt dislocated, out of place. What remained of my humanity was pushing me to make the most of all the companionship life could offer, but even then, even if I were surrounded by friends and with a smile on my face, my rooted sense of solitude made me feel rather overwhelmed, as well as guilty, for being increasingly less sociable. And I had achieved it, I was alone, then why the hell was I so desperate to speak with someone? I had my gaze lost in the urban landscape which, in turn, went to lose itself amid its lights and shadows while I was thinking for an answer…

Fuck! What had I become? Where would my happiness now lie if in solitude I felt empty and in company distressed?

There startled us —me and my sleep— a blinding light and the much more enthusiastic driver's voice. It seems I hadn't had enough with sleeping in the plane and I had just debated shamelessly aloud, eyelids closed, in my dreams, with myself, in the car.

'It's not words that you are looking for,' was the taxi driver saying with passionate voice, 'you are looking for what underlies them, the comprehension of another human being, since it's clear that your conscience disapproves of what you thought, and still now sense, was the right thing to do. How ridiculous these contradictions wrestling inside you! Your conscience condemns you and you condemn her back. Anyway, that will be twenty-three pounds, sir.'

I handed over to him the first note my fingers found in my wallet, and got out of that taxi without either replying nor taking the change; the door closed itself somehow and the taxi drove away. I was perplexed, I did not know there were in the world people able to talk like this, I simply wasn't ready for such a high-level conversation. In books one can find marvellous texts but which belong to those conscientious authors who, with time, weighed their words and patiently put them together. Who can know that much about a person, having heard so little? Besides, who can find the ideal words in a few minutes, even seconds, while driving through the jammed roads of the English capital? He must be someone that knows all the answers, someday I will also know them myself and speak like him.

When I broke out of the trance I was in, and looked around, I realised I was in Trafalgar Square. What a pleasant sensation! I was in London, far away from the suffocating heat left behind in Mallorca; but summer had just begun and so the city wasn't as cold as I would have liked it to be. It wasn't nighttime yet, but it wouldn't be too long until the sun got completely hidden behind some London monument. The air smelled of rain and grey colours, people were speaking the language of music… I had the feeling of being where I was meant to be. The fountain was simply beautiful, neither magnificent nor extravagant nor simple, nor dark nor corny, beautiful. Three statues were standing above the shallow and clear water of its pool, a pool in the shape of a quadrangle with two ellipses superimposed in the form of a cross. The statue in the middle consisted of a wide circular pedestal a good six-foot in height, at the top of which a proportioned basin stood and sustained a steady jet of water upwards. The two other statues were placed one at each end of the ellipse lying parallel to the main road and the Square's layout. These statues were made of bronze and represented a triton and a mermaid surrounded by dolphins, from whose snouts water was spouting. And there were two fountains, each with its pool and three statues, one next to the other. And between them and the road, there raised skywards a column as tall as any, surrounded on its base by four bronze lions. I didn't give them much importance, not even to the statue that crowned the enormous column… column… Corinthian, to say something. Anyway, the bronze man at the top was a forgotten character, that's how it should be for all those who forsook the world of the living. I circled the left pool contemplating closely the statues of marine features. When I had already walked around half a pool, I sat sideways on its edge. I stroked the water and looked at it, with exhausted eyes, when I stopped stroking and some of it trickled down my hand; thin, big and graceful, yes, but delicate. I remember, thumbing the tip of my fingers, when I practiced climbing and my hands were strong and rough. My fingers, notwithstanding, had always been long and slender, because of which I was always asked if I played the piano and to which I would always reply that I did not. The first few times it happened, I would picture myself in front of a piano and subsequently shrug my shoulders not knowing what to think of such a strange image. But people kept asking and at a turning point I began to take it as a compliment. Thus, the image of me caressing a melody on so iconic an instrument no longer manifested itself in my mind so strangely, rather I enjoyed imagining myself sitting in an empty hall before a black grand piano, watching how my fingers seemed to come to life brisk on its keys. And the image was so diaphanous… I felt powerless at not being able to hear what I was carrying within. As the sole spectator of a silent melody I used to open my notebook and write what my soul had to say, a phrase, a paragraph or a couple of pages. Then I would read my words aloud trying to imagine how they would sound if these were music, if my voice were the piano's and my writing, a score…

I recognise it's useless to try to hear among my words the chords of a gentle melody, but on finishing my reading I am overcome by a familiar feeling, and still strange, that is blend of happiness, pain, love and passion, that same feeling that invades us when listening to a killer melody whose composition strained the compositor to death. That feeling is life, it is all, since all that is beautiful and worthy can be understood as a guffaw, a wound that hurts, a heartfelt kiss or a muscular boner. By the same token, comprehension can't be listened to, let alone be read. To comprehend one must feel!

Leaving the notebook open on my lap, I raised my eyes in search of inspiration. Water was flowing, raising and falling non-stop. Its chant couldn't be imitated by a piano but the sensation I experienced when listening to its ups and downs could be captured on paper, as if in a jar, so reality wouldn't poison its content and, later, when seeing myself exposed to its dearth, I could open the lid and find in there every single drop of the chant once heard. This is what I used to do, as well, after a turbulent dream, with the hope of untangling it even if just a little. Nevertheless, many times were those when I would take notes in a dream only for the awakening to take them all away, even their memory. Would I find my notes tomorrow morning?

I went straight to sit at the left pool's edge, encircling first half of it while contemplating closely the fountains: symbol of fluency, uprise, downfall and summit again. Symbol of birth, the continuous, of eternal return…

VII

I was tired from the journey and the long hours with little to no sleep, the clothes I was wearing didn't appear to me as marvellous as they used to, they belonged to a past life and now looked old and dirty. The National Gallery was open and there was no better occasion to visit a gallery than with my current state of insomnia, perhaps with my delirium I would see the paintings come to life, I thought. As I was going up the steps, though, I realised this was not the right moment, my legs felt very heavy; well, truth be told, my whole body felt heavy. I took off my leather jacket as he who takes off from his back a corpse he's been carrying for days through the desert, and went into the museum regardless.

'Excuse me,' I said to the young receptionist, 'at what time does the museum close?'

'It's eight o'clock now, so the museum will close in an hour. You should come another day with some more time, you can see real treasures in this gallery.'

'I know, I have one right in front of me,' I said while winking at her and walked off, since I didn't expect any other reply than a pair of blushing cheeks or a lazy smile for such an unimaginative compliment. I was wrong.

'Wait a second, sir. I've just finished my shift. I normally enjoy a little walk through the gallery at this time of the day and go to see my favourite paintings. Perhaps you'd like to join me?'

Low in energy and not in the right mood, I could do nothing but to be honest with her:

'Right now I have a conflict of interests: on the one hand I would love to walk with you wherever you go, but on the other hand I don't think I would be a good companion this evening. You see, I've been two days without sleep nor taking a shower. Besides, today I have not yet had a bite to eat; I feel hungry and tired and yet I have neither appetite nor desire to sleep. All I want is a hot shower and a clean t-shirt.'

'I always take my little stroll alone, I admit that at the beginning I enjoyed saving this time to myself but for a few weeks I've been feeling like sharing it with someone,' said she with her gaze lost in a landscape painting, as if the canvas were a window, before turning her eyes to me and charitably sparing me a few more words. 'I see you are a little the worse for wear but it doesn't bother me at all and...' she paused and bent forwards to smell my neck, 'you actually smell lovely for not having had a shower in two days. Come on, come with me, don't be like the man who wanted chicken for dinner,' said she and began to walk away; she took four strides and turned around. 'If you come with me I promise I'll help you get a t-shirt.'

After listening to the phrase "the man who wanted chicken for dinner" I felt as discombobulated as… as… as if all of a sudden the whole world had become pink and the sea were an enormous strawberry milkshake. I ran after her, for her strides were swift and she was already about to disappear among the crowd; not giving me time to think, I was forced to accept her proposal.

'Who is that man who wanted chicken for dinner?' I asked when I reached her, with my breathing slightly quickened from the sprint.

'Oh, I'm sorry,' she laughed. 'I sometimes do that. I like to construct sentences with no sense,' said she without giving it any importance, when it had actually struck me like a thunderbolt.

'What?' I had just noticed that in the restaurants of my pink world only candyfloss was being served. 'You can't just leave me wondering like that, what happened to the man that wanted chicken for dinner? Who is he? The protagonist from some bizarre news story or does he belong to some kinky English tale?' she couldn't contain herself and roared with laughter. It was one of those contagious laughs so I laughed along with her, first out of empathy and then kept on laughing intoxicated by the feeling I had made an absurd comment, since I didn't see any other reason for such merriment. When I calmed down and gathered my wits I insisted once again, 'The character of a cult movie?' Then the laughter subsided and her face, more serene, returned to normal. I thought I had hit the nail on the head and, right after, the laughter burst out once more. I, however, did no longer laugh. Not because I was upset or anything like that, but because now I was looking at her properly, I had not previously noticed her skin, fair white and fine, her hands, elegant and slim, her cheeks as pink as my disconcerting world; I had not noticed how her uniform was shaping her hourglass figure, nor her eyes...

'Is there something the matter?' She said when noticing my gaze anchored on her.

You are beautiful, I thought, but my mouth babbled something of the style 'the no sleeping, that disconcerts me', always fearful of my words.

'I hope you are not upset, I didn't mean to laugh at you, I simply enjoy a bit too much seeing how people react to my sentences.'

'And how is it they normally react?'

'Normally they don't even notice them. It's difficult to find somebody who listens, but even more so is to find somebody capable of recognising what is unknown to himself. I'm sorry, I think I have not expressed myself properly…'

'At high school my Philosophy teacher once played a video of some guys passing a basketball to each other. Before playing the video the teacher challenged us to count the total number of passes they would do. When the video came to an end everybody knew the answer but no one had seen the bear…'

'The bear?' She interrupted me but it did not irritate me, that just meant she was listening carefully. She had actually noticed the bear.

'Well, it seems that while these guys were passing the basketball to each other, another guy wearing a bear costume entered the scene; and he did not enter it stealthily, no, he went across the others while moonwalking and doing all sorts of flashy, silly things. The teacher explained that as we didn't expect to see any bear, we simply didn't see it. Is this what you meant? That we don't see what we don't expect to see?' She wasn't saying anything and the silence was stretching on too much. 'Well, applied to this case that would mean that we don't hear what we don't expect to hear. Were we to look for a more general conclusion, we could say… that we ignore every idea that is not preconceived', intoning this last sentence as if it were more of a question rather than an affirmation.

'I think that the general conclusion has a few "weaknesses"…' marking she, too, with cheeky fingers, her word with quotation marks, 'but right now I'm incapable of phrasing it any better. All in all, you and I understand each other, no more words required. What do you think about this painting?' Without noticing she had led me through stairs, corridors and rooms, and we were now standing before an oil painting whose title stated: *The Fighting Temeraire tugged to her last berth to be broken up* by William Turner.

The painting was magnificent. It showed a small steamer tugging, as the title said, a vessel as majestic as those seen in pirate movies. The scene was placed in an evening in which you could see the sun coming down in a fired up sunset. In a certain way death was represented in it, the vessel portrayed breaking its last waves to the berth. But it wasn't a disagreeable end, it was an honourable and unavoidable closure to what I imagined had been a prosperous life. The sun setting reminding us the twilight of *The Fighting Temeraire*, its colours celebrating life, warmth and beauty… Every stroke transmitting to its observer a feeling of peace, like the one felt when ending a long journey: a blend of satisfaction and exhaustion that, together with a calm conscience, could well put a grown man to sleep. The ship had survived storms and battles, had taken full possession of seas as it ploughed through them. And now it was retiring, leaving its great legacy to future generations. Who could aspire to more when breathing their last? I wasn't dying but at that moment I had the certainty I would feel something similar when doing so.

All this I had to say about one of her favourite paintings and, even then, I only told her I thought it was very pretty and asked her, right after, which were the other works she would take me to see. I could feel how my so dull a comment had disappointed her, how I had torn to shreds the illusory image she had formed of me. She said that was the only stop of her routine stroll, that it was her favourite painting —now it would also be mine—, but she said so already without a pinch of the grace she had addressed me with before. I had ripped the spell open; her eyes turned off. An uncomfortable and tense silence came into being, one of those which no word can aggravate, so in a desperate attempt I said the first thing that crossed my mind:

'Before we say goodbye and never see each other again, could you tell me what was that about the man who wanted chicken for dinner?' Her eyes turned back on and her smile flourished with one dimple on each cheek.

'You are not the only one with whom I've laughed at my sentences with no sense, but I've never found anyone before so anxious to know the story they hide.'

'Is there one?' I asked, making it sound as if it were a plea.

'Not yet, but I will see if I can do something about it,' she winked at me and looked at the time on her phone, 'now it's half past eight. I'll tell you what we're going to do, you wanted a clean t-shirt, didn't you?' I nodded with my head. 'Then let's go to the gift shop and I'll tell you my plan in the meantime.'

She told me what she had in mind, without slowing down her pace, and upon arriving at the shop she left me to my fate. It didn't take me long until I saw the one I had to buy. It was a t-shirt of a greyish white colour and decorated with an outlandish drawing by some artist called Michael Landy. On the label, the drawing's title: *Saint Jerome Hearing the Trumpet of the Last Judgement*. Puzzling, like the girl that had just told me to meet her at half past ten in the English pub Walkers of Whitehall, assuring me that, by then, she would have a story for the man who wanted chicken for dinner. I was sure my newly bought t-shirt also had its own story, but I would worry about this one some other time.

VIII

I still remember my first shower in London. With no more luggage than the clean t-shirt inside a National Gallery plastic bag, I walked into the hall of the first hotel I found. It was excessively luxurious and I could only afford one night, but I was carrying thousands of kilometres on my back, I was worn out and meant to have a date in half an hour, so that would be the night. I disbursed the amount of four hundred pounds at the reception desk and went up to room 201.

The bedroom was… the bed was… The truth is that I don't remember very well how the room was, but what I do remember is all that crossed my mind before going out. I threw the old t-shirt to the bin and shaved carefully as I always used to before a date. My hand was trembling a little, but I did not cut myself, and right after finishing I went into the shower. Water had always had a calming and cleansing power over me, but that night was different. The drops of water began to bite me as soon as I turned on the tap, the noise they made when falling and clashing against my body was rumbling in my head as if beats on a drum and, as if I didn't think those were enough, from my eyes came out more drops. I brought my hands to my head and grabbed my hair and pulled on it, my hands slid down then to my face and slid further down on my body pressing it with strength. I felt the desire to pull my skin off but I didn't find the courage. I crossed my arms over my chest, seizing both shoulders to keep my body from exploding, but it was ever-expanding and I couldn't do anything about it, my hands were inevitably sliding down scratching my chest. My skin wasn't burning nor was I lacking air, I didn't feel any physical pain but I could sense the walls caving in over my body, naked and rosy from the steaming water. Still with shampoo on my hair I turned the tap off and left the bathroom in haste, soaking wet, ready to jump off the balcony. Little could my bare feet do when they stepped on the floor tiles soaked with the suds that my hair was dripping, they simply slipped and I fell flat on my back. The blow to my head, despite leaving me stunned and dizzy, was loud rather than painful and served to calm me down. I remained stretched out on the floor for a couple of minutes, motionless, thoughtlessly contemplating the salmon colour of the ceiling. Slightly calmer I idly got up and sat down on the corner of the bed with my legs open and my arms hanging in between them, like a boxer after the toughest round. I was looking down all crestfallen when I noticed the floor tiles curiously placed: all of them were white and square but with two different sizes, the smaller ones being enclosed by the bigger ones, four times their size. The joints owned the black hue of the night, highlighted by the chequered whiteness; they weren't broad, neither were they thin. Altogether it formed a simple pattern that, as ironic as this could be, brought to one's mind the idea of complexity. And I observed them while my thoughts, running free, ran towards that memory of mine in which I had stared at a tiled floor for as long. I looked at my notebook and began to recall…

I had acquired it three months ago when I went to a stationery shop to buy a new calculator, since my old one had stopped working. But when the shop assistant asked me whether I had checked if the problem was not the batteries, I replied that I hadn't. Luckily for me, although in an embarrassing way, she turned out to be right —that blessed and scrawny clerk—, which saved me fifteen euros at least.

Merry with the sensation of relief of those who get relieved of an absurd expense, I decided to leave her to her job and walk about the shop. I was moving slowly along its corridors walled up with solid shelves full of canvasses, brushes, aquarelles, office supplies and unnamable doohickeys. There were even walls erected with sheets of paper and poster boards of hundreds of colours, each bundle of them mimicking the sturdiness and sobriety of well-placed red bricks.

The strip lighting lit all the room uniformly which, leaving everything at the sight of the most distracted observer, made it difficult to imagine that the shop could possess any mystery at all. Anyone could go in and see the ingenuousness with which people bought. How many of those canvasses had been left to wither for lack of inspiration and dedication, or for the mere fact of having to study for a History exam? Or even worse, how many of them had been left unpacked in their plastic, condemned to be unpainted and never be fulfilled? Or even worse, how many canvasses had been scrawled in a rush due to lack of time?

In the meantime the clerk was focused on her task, still stuck in the initial phase, trying to take off the calculator's batteries cover, which was fixed to its base by four minuscule screws barely perceptible. Why would they make it so difficult? And, as expected, one of the screws fell to the floor —at least that was what she said— following Murphy's law —that was me who thought it— which states "anything that can go wrong, will go wrong." I didn't agree with it, too pessimistic for my taste, but every time something like that happened to me I was reminded of that extravagant law and was cheered up by its existence. 'Murphy's law' I used to say to myself and smiled in silence no matter what the situation.

'Where has it fallen?'

'It should be somewhere in front of the counter, young man,' she said in a serious and somewhat mocking tone, as if she had ulterior motives or were actually thinking about something else.

I supposed the best thing to do would be to forget about it, after all everybody is entitled to speak in their own way. I told her to screw off the rest, that I would look for the dropped one in the meantime. My engineer brain told me that to look for it in a two meters radius would be enough but I was wrong, again: neither calculators expire after two years nor everything that falls follows a logical trajectory. So I decided to extend my searching area to the whole main aisle and, when I was running my eyes over it for the fifth time, the clerk had already finished replacing the batteries.

'Let it go, young man. The cover looks quite secure even with one screw missing.'

My first reaction was to give up and walk slowly to the counter with my eyes scanning the floor in the hope I would discern, at the very last minute, a dark glint among the white tiles. I discerned nothing. I took out a ten euros note to pay and put it right back inside my pocket.

'Do you mind if I keep searching a little bit more?' I said with the naivety of a knocked out boxer that affirms he can still beat his strong opponent.

'It won't be me who will put a halt to your search, young man,' she said, followed by a monologue that glorified all those who seek.

It couldn't have fallen in any of the parallel aisles, that was impossible, but after looking through the shelves of that corridor, the main one, I decided to step out of logic and try my luck.

The old clerk began to speak. From her low tone and the degree of abstraction of her words she seemed not to be talking to me so much as to be thinking out loud. Whichever were her intentions, she wouldn't stop murmuring, just loud enough so I could hear her while wandering about those aisles.

'People long so anxiously for the search that sometimes bury and abandon something very precious to them just to feel the desire to thrust themselves into the quest to recover the treasure they left behind…'

With every second that passed with the screw undiscovered I was more determined to find it. I was so focused that her voice became a sort of white noise.

'Every object that is longed to be found possesses part of the seeker's soul…'

I turned left at the end of the last shelf and there it was, camouflaged in the corner, the most remote point from the counter. 'Impossible!' would have thought anyone unable to imagine a millimetric screw fall from a four foot counter and end up, after crossing or jumping over two fully stocked shelves, in a corner ten metres far from its origin.

She kept beating around the bush, ignoring what my eyes had seen, 'Where will what is forever lost go? Will it cross some sort of threshold towards an unknown dimension?'

Had I crossed that threshold? Raising my eyes a little above where the screw was lying, I saw, in a dark nook, the mystery of the shop…

I kept looking at my notebook. It did look mysterious; I walked towards the desk where it lay open, attracted by that same spell I felt when I saw it for the first time. I wrote in it the first thing that crossed my mind while my tears were plunging on the paper. When I read it I saw it was my suicide note. It was very brief, it could be read out loud without the need of pausing to catch breath, not even once. Its scarce words, whilst perturbing and troubling, were not depressing or disheartening, but reflected instead the author's desire to live and how that desire was eating him away. I stripped off the sheet, crumpling it and pulling it out, and put it in the inner pocket of my jacket. My thoughts always turned out to be more complex when transcribing them on the page, and reading those helped me, afterwards, to penetrate deeper into my soul. Then, wondering why I didn't speak in the manner I wrote, I could felt my own voice overflowing:

'Tonight I will dive into death, that's it, I'm going out into the streets and I'm going to shout! Tonight I won't eat anything until I can roar as a lion, not drink a thing until my own thirst gets me drunk. Tonight I will not smoke any cigar for the same air will be my smoke, the music will be the deafening noise of a crammed city, the stars will hang from the sky as every other night, but I'm not going to look upwards to check whether they are hidden behind the clouds or shine more than yesterday, I will not write down any note nor will I look sideways at any woman. I will run through the streets and take everything that's in my way never fearing whose hands I craved to snatch from. Tonight I'm going to be myself, tonight I'm going to be myself and no one else!'

And with that fighting cry I came out of the hotel and of my shell.

IX

I arrived half an hour late but there she was, sitting at the bar drinking a one finger dram of what seemed to be a single malt. She was sipping it slowly, savouring it. I delayed my date five minutes more, which I spent studying her from the entrance corner. She was still wearing, to my surprise, the museum's uniform and her hair modestly upswept with a pony tail; she had her legs crossed and her glance lost among the liqueur bottles behind the bar. Her blonde locks were inciting sin but her face wasn't impish nor lustful, as might be expected, instead she showed a face of innocent features. It is said that the Devil, trying to go unnoticed, hides behind this sort of masks, but I wonder: If what is beautiful and pure shows itself such as it is, beautiful and pure, how can we, at first sight, differentiate it from the masked horror? She stood up and made ready to pay the bill when, without an answer to my question, my doubt and I sat down next to her.

'Two pints of your best local ale,' to the bartender. 'You look very pretty, I'm sorry I'm not up to your mark' to her.

'Hello,' she spat, surprised that I had addressed her.

'Don't you recognise me? Two hours ago, in the museum…'

'Oh, I'm sorry, I was already convinced you wouldn't show up,' she seemed annoyed at my delay.

'Well, I'm here now. You won't allow this poor vagabond to drink by himself, will you?' I said, changing my euphoric countenance into the parody of a repentant one.

'No, but I did actually have a drink by myself while I was waiting for you, so if you want me to stay you will have to compensate me someway.'

'I'm getting you a beer, isn't that enough?' I said so because the script required it, but I was eager to please her whatever her petition was.

'Well, it is a start but no, it's not enough. Besides, it occurred to me, while I was waiting,' she would not forget easily, 'that as this night is all about stories, you will have to tell me something interesting if you want me to tell you what happened to the man who wanted chicken for dinner. Normally, people excuse themselves after arriving late and explain to those who they were supposed to meet what has delayed them. You haven't done any of that and I wonder why,' her mind was incredibly agile analysing people and what she said seemed to have a lot of sense, but she was wrong; I simply never apologised nor gave excuses for insignificant little trifles, I consider it to be an unhealthy habit; therefore I limited myself to raise a brow in reply. 'I'm not asking you to open up your soul nor to tell me your life story, I'm just asking you to tell me why you've been,' she looked at the watch on her wrist, 'thirty-seven minutes late. Come on, tell me, you have to compensate my wait,' she insisted again, intrigued even more by the reluctant countenance that I had just projected. 'Reveal the mystery or on the contrary I will go,' and she said so with confidence, assured that I would accept. She was right, but I just half accepted; although I wasn't willing to let her go, I didn't want for anything in this world to talk about my last hours.

'Ok, ok. Let me think…'

'No! I don't want you to have time to think of a lie.'

'Calm down, I'm just trying to choose my words…'

'The words of deceit… I know them well. Just tell me!' That seemed to be her method, she hurried people so that they just had time to follow their instincts or to tell the truth. Later on I would ask her if that method really existed because, sincerely, it was effective; it had already worked in the National Gallery to make me go with her and it worked again, 'Tell me!'

'I died! Are you happy now? I died! Is this what you really wanted to hear?' I said, irate, with a voice I couldn't control.

'And what does it feel like to die?' She asked me without blinking. I was waiting for an awkward silence or, at least, some reply asking for explanations for my behaviour. I dithered a few seconds, puzzled by how she had received my demons so openly, and I told her, since her question-answer well deserved it. Moreover, apart from her method, the bewilderment her words provoked in me had brought me to a quasi state of hypnosis.

'It's not really what I expected,' I then went on to explain in detail what her favourite painting had really made me feel, as well as the reflections I had extracted from it regarding how the experience of dying might be. I described to her, next, how I had suffered death that very night, 'I felt out of me and conscious of my acts, all at the same time, while I was hearing moaning, inside, a voice that wasn't mine. Those moans soon became drowned sobs of panic and, afterwards, screams of pain. The screams ceased, silence, peace… That's dying, to suffer such an intense and heartbreaking pain that it seems to be someone else's. And then you realise that you never have suffered really, that the body you inhabit is but the legacy of a tormented soul and that, as sons are doomed to pay the debts of their fathers, equally are you obliged to amend any of its past mistakes. That is, if you really really want to be yourself.

'Wait, let me get this straight. So you are telling me that you have died, that you have been born again and that yet you are still not yourself, is that right?'

'In some way. Before trying to understand me you have to first accept the premise that no one is fully oneself and no one ever manages to be so. There are two kinds of people: the ones who deceive themselves and the ones who aspire to find themselves. I wasn't searching before, I was scared of my voice and used to silence it, but now I'm not afraid anymore, I'm ready to go along the path, whichever this may be, so long as it brings me a little closer to the finish line.'

'But, sweetheart,' she said with the greatest tenderness any woman could express, 'this is not what we call dying, what you've experienced has a name and this name is change, some are more steady and others more sudden, but changes anyhow. I know that I can't imagine the vertigo you might have suffered in falling to that abysm; I don't know its depth for I don't know how profoundly you are capable of imagining. But don't dramatise, it doesn't flatter you.' The phrase ended and I fell head over heels for her.

'Perhaps you are right,' it was the only thing I could mutter without shedding a tear; I think she perceived it and so changed the subject, aware of my emotional response.

'Well, let's forget about deep conversations. Do you know that those parts of the brain you use when imagining yourself doing something are actually the self-same parts you use when doing that something?' She said as if a tongue-twister. I shook my head, 'I heard it for the first time on TV when a famous Formula One driver was explaining his training routine. One of his day-to-day exercises consisted of sitting down and imagining himself driving the next circuit he had to compete on. I think that in this case some advantage can be taken from this phenomenon; in fact, most people apply it continuously in their lives, but they apply it wrongly; they sate their wish for travelling while seated in front of a screen watching some documentary about a foreign country, or they believe to be having sex while masturbating in solitude and ejaculating on a crumpled paper napkin, they watch films and read books to satisfy their hunger for adventure, they listen and read others' words and recite them as if these were theirs without taking the bother of seeking their own voice,' hers seemed the voice of a radio with low signal. I pushed myself to listen carefully to it but the only thing I achieved was to grasp scattered words, without understanding the meaning of their ensemble.

Tired of sinking more than sailing, I took a large swig of my pint and interrupted her to ask about the man who wanted chicken for dinner.

'Where is all this coming from now? Didn't you have to tell me the story of the man who wanted chicken for dinner?'

'I have begun the story and you haven't even realised it. If you don't mind, I will continue…'

'Wait a minute,' I interrupted her again, 'excuse me if I seem old-fashioned but I would like to know the title of your tale.'

'Oh, yes, sorry. It's good you asked since I have a perfect one, are you ready?' I nodded, '*Chicken, harlots and muffins*. What do you think?'

'I think that I won't be able to sleep tonight if I don't get to find out what happened to the man who wanted chicken for dinner' I said it sincerely and she knew it.

'In that case I'better continue: We won't fill our stomach imagining that we eat a chicken, but if we are able to imagine ourselves buying or hunting the chicken and later see ourselves cooking it, perhaps we could in fact put an end to our appetite. But I could see a flaw in this technique: the Formula One driver wasn't taking into consideration, among other factors, the other drivers, the performance of his team of engineers, the weather conditions nor his physical and mental state on the day of the race. And that is exactly what happened to the character of the story I'm about to narrate: he didn't contemplate all the possibilities.

'Imagine that the hungry character decides to undertake his most studied plan towards a roast chicken. He gets up from the sofa and goes to the butcher's. The butcher's might be closed due to a family emergency or the walk-in freezer might be broken, its provider might have not been able to restock them or, even worse, imagine that our hungry character doesn't even arrive at the shop, that he falls down the stairs or is hit by a car or something. But, well, let's suppose that our hungry character comes back home unharmed and with his whole chicken, he's an expert cook so he marinades it properly, while his mouth waters, and puts it in the oven at the ideal temperature; he is not forgetful but he sets up the alarm anyway to sound one hour later and, this way, make sure not to burn it. Everything seems to go as planned, do you think he will get to eat it? Relax, I promise you I'm not going to run him over nor will the kitchen gas explode while he's cooking some fries, I'm not going to let anything this frivolous happen to him, but remember: the possibilities are still infinite. Okay, it turns out that the hour wears away fast and before the beep of the alarm sounds he's already in front of the oven, he opens it and smells its aroma; it will be delicious, he thinks. He could already eat it but he likes it more cooked, so decides to let it roast for another fifteen minutes, he's anxious but also convinced that it's worth the wait. He spends all the time, minute after minute, in front of the oven, until in the final sixty seconds count the phone rings. He goes running to take the call, it's his best friend, 50 seconds, who greets him as great friends do, with time, affection and some swearwords but he can only think about the chicken, 30 seconds, he replies laconically so that his colleague can say whatever he had to say, 25 seconds, he invites our character to have dinner at his home and, before explaining the plan with more detail, our man interrupts him, 5 seconds, "I'm sorry but I've already cooked my dinner, talk tomorrow, fella," *ding-ding*, he hangs up, the chicken is ready!

'He conquers the first bite, the chicken is tasty, the skin is crispy and the meat tender, it melts in the mouth. He keeps eating unhurriedly but soon gets distracted, tomorrow is Sunday, the only day it is worthwhile to get up early and go out for breakfast. He keeps gobbling it down unconsciously, not really savouring his so long-awaited dinner, tomorrow is the day he says to himself. She will be sitting at her usual table, next to the furthest window from the comings and goings of the entrance, she will eat a big chocolate muffin, taking small pieces with her hand and bringing them to her mouth, slowly, while with her eyes she devours one of those strange books, of worn out covers and yellowish pages. She might even let out a shriek of laughter or shed a tear, she might bring the book close to her chest and sigh moved by a phrase of great literary genius. She will lengthen as much as she can that sweet moment of letters and chocolate ordering a mug of mocha, but not without first eating the muffin crumbs left on the wrapping paper, picking them up delicately with a damp fingertip. She will keep reading, drinking a sip in between pages, and so on, and so forth till the end of one or the other, the book or the breakfast, then he will approach her and tell her that he couldn't help fixing his eyes on her, on her peculiar Sunday morning ritual and how in this fixation he was seduced by her grace, her literary tastes, her mysterious solitude, her beauty… The dish is empty except for the fowl's bones, and his stomach full except for the gap reserved for tomorrow's breakfast. He goes to bed nervous and falls asleep rehearsing what he could say to her and how he would say it.

'He wakes up relaxed, not knowing that outside his sleep the cruelest nightmare is stalking him, that which one can never wake up from. He would have got dressed with his best shirt and his shiniest shoes, but he has studied her many mornings and thinks he knows her tastes well, he intuits his faithful boots and a modest jumper will have a greater effect on her. This is the morning, he says to himself, this is the morning. He goes out into the streets and starts walking; on his way to the bar he stumbles over his feet a few times, his mind is not focused. When opening the door he realises he's really in love. He's nervous and excessively excited, he has forced himself to believe he was doing all that in order to face his shyness more than for love, but at the moment of truth he can't pretend such a folly, two emptied Bloody Maries at five past ten in the morning corroborate it. At a quarter past ten he starts feeling the weight of the alcohol on his empty stomach, its warmth on his cheeks and a light loss of control over his actions; he asks the waiter for a large cup of coffee in order to be more serene and, why not?, a muffin like those his lover-to-be always asked for. It tastes like glory, he eats it in no more than five bites in spite of its enormous size. He feels en even greater urge to meet her now, how the hell does she manage to eat it crumb by crumb, and so slowly? Half past ten, her estimated time of arrival.

'Half past ten, this time at night. He opens his apartment's door after struggling ten minutes with the key and the lock. Rose, which was how he had baptised the nameless girl he was so madly in love with, today of all days, had encountered all the issues that could befall upon her. First she had overslept, after she couldn't find any taxi or her car didn't start, maybe she missed the bus or the train from a place with bad connections. At midday he thought that perhaps she had stumbled into old friendships that had entertained her and had forced her to have breakfast with them in a seedy bar; poor girl he thought. He still had the hope of seeing her crossing the cafe and sitting down at her favourite table to eat something. But at two o'clock she wasn't there yet and he supposed she might have preferred to come later for some tea and so he waited for her, sitting in the same place getting up not even once to go to the toilet. This way, as he was trying to convince himself that sooner or later she would walk as if on a catwalk before him with her usual grace and a book under her arms, he was alternating brandies to calm down and coffees to be alert. This is the afternoon, he said to himself, this is the afternoon. They ended up kicking him out at half past nine; they were closing at eleven o'clock but it was hours ago that he had broken the delicate equilibrium of alcohol and caffeine, and his inebriation had started to scare both staff and clientele; he wouldn't stop crying out for a chocolate muffin and telling him they had run out only made his cries louder: "A chocolate muffin!"

'He enters his apartment and goes straight to the bathroom for the first time in twelve hours. In that moment of calm in which one lifts a weight off oneself he starts to see things with more optimism, not everything is lost. She might have hit a snag, had a commitment she couldn't miss or her mother had died. Something very important must have happened to make her miss her so appreciated moment. Besides, hers was an act she carried out in the most absolute intimacy with some sort of roguery, her naughty gaze gave her away. No one abandons such a habit just like that. But it doesn't matter much, in case her mother had died, they can bury her during the week and all is sorted, on Sunday she will be ready to attend her unexpected date with a mysterious suitor.

'He reaches for the mobile phone he left early this morning on the entrance sideboard and reads his friend's message: "I've been calling you countless times, call me back whenever you can, we need to talk." He phones him right away fearing a tragedy might have happened, but when his colleague answers immediately he realises that it was all good news, for his friend at least.

'"What a dinner you missed, my friend! I've met the love of my life."

'He had always criticised girls for their chit-chatting about this sort of things, but the truth is that they had done exactly the same since they discovered the female sex in their adolescence, chasing girls together. He doesn't feel like talking about love affairs, but it's his best friend and so he makes as if he were interested in whatever he had to say.

'"Tell me, tell me, motherfucker," motherfucker? He couldn't hide those two, perhaps ten, drinks too many.

'"Have you been drinking? Well, never mind, what I wanted to tell you is that I had organised a dinner for my workmates but later they suggested everybody should bring a plus one in order to get to know each other better. They said it three days ago but what with being absent-minded, organising the dinner and the whole caboodle I didn't tell you till the very last minute…"

'"Don't worry," his friend seemed to be repentant, "you know I don't care, just stop apologising and go straight to the interesting part," he said laconically and with all the seriousness he could pretend, for his friend had indeed smelled his breath through the phone line.

'"Ok, pay attention. So the ugly copy-girl comes and brings along her cousin of infinite legs and seductive face. What a woman! She sat next to me and we talked all dinner and, do you know what she replied when I asked her if she wanted dessert?" his voice had increasingly taken a high-pitched tone while he was narrating his night —as if he were connecting with his inner child—, he always did so when telling a blue joke or talking about some recent mischief.

Our character knew there was no point in answering since his friend's impatience would push him to answer his own question. "Her words were: I am a cheap harlot, if you can promise me an old book from your shelves, a chocolate muffin and a huge mug of mocha in the morning, then I shall be all yours tonight."

'He felt he stopped feeling. The phone smashed to the floor but his friend didn't realise what was going on and so kept on narrating. The last he heard, while collapsing on the sofa, were his friend's laughs and his comment: "And now imagine she whispers it into your ear while placing her hand on your groin! I'm not lying to you…" He couldn't bear to listen any longer and hung up horrified. He was gone, no thought was rolling in his mind, and when the phone started ringing again he remained still. The voicemail took the message, his death sentence. He walked as an automaton to the balcony, leaned on the rail. This is the night, he says to himself, this is the night. And he leapt into the void before Sunday had time to end, as he had planned in a way, though he didn't find soft breasts at its bottom but the concrete ground of a most defeated hero.'

'Why a most defeated hero? I mean, his defeat is obvious but why the emphasis? The man who wanted chicken for dinner did have his chicken after all.' Said I, teasingly but also with genuine intrigue. The tale had been incredible and her way of telling it even more, but I sensed something ulterior in the way she had phrased that last bit, so I asked her before saying how much I had enjoyed it.

'I'm glad you asked ,' she really seemed to be waiting for it. 'He did everything in his hands in order to achieve his two goals, put his heart into it and even managed to accomplish one of them, but he failed precisely for that same reason. Had he been bone-idle and accepted eating anything for dinner and refused trying to conquer his lady, perhaps he would have obtained, at the end of the night, everything he had wished for.'

'What do you mean by everything? You don't mean that… It cannot be! Which was the ill-fated voicemail?' I could imagine the ending but I had to hear it from her own voice.

'As it couldn't be any other way,' she said, progressively attenuating her voice while approaching her face to mine, 'his chatty friend finished sinking the blade of the sword into his skin when added that, besides,' her voice was barely a whisper when her lips brushed my ear, 'he had missed a delicious roast chicken.'

'No!' I shouted after such a surprising end. It struck me as great films do after a denouement so plausible as unexpected.

I asked for two drams of Cardhu while fascination and excitement coursed through my body. We remained quiet for a few minutes, the time it took the waiter to serve our drinks, reflecting on the misfortune of her character. We drank them in one gulp and asked for two more beers to comment on the story.

'I already knew you were something out of the ordinary but now, well, what can I say? Your imagination is limitless,' I couldn't believe that she had made up that tale in scarcely two hours, that she had narrated it with such confidence and, moreover, that she was so coherent with what she meant during the first words we exchanged: don't be like the man who wanted chicken for dinner. At last I understood its meaning but if I had to explain it to someone else I would find myself in a tight spot, so I asked her for a precise answer. 'Then, when you told me not to be like the man who wanted chicken for dinner, what were you trying to say exactly?'

'What I wanted to say was…' she, too, seemed to have difficulties expressing it, 'what I wanted to say was that you should do whatever you fancy in the moment, but also that you should not allow your fancies to stop you from going with the flow every now and then, for however controlled you want to have things, however careful you may be, you never know where your steps might bring you. Goals lead to failure, failure leads to regret and this latter, to the tomb,' said she with a charming insecurity.

'Then, we shouldn't have goals, is that what you are saying?' I insisted on needling her a little.

'Yes, but not as a way of living… we shouldn't let ourselves be dazzled by them…' What a tangle she had inside her head. 'No, it's not exactly that either… I don't know how to say it,' she said, angry with herself; after having prepared her story so carefully and narrated it so finely, she was annoyed when she couldn't find the right words for a spot-on conclusion.

'Don't worry, you artful storyteller, I think that your reasoning has a few weaknesses,' I said, with mockery, making an allusion to one of her many commentaries that caught my attention in The National Gallery, 'but right now I'm unable to express it any better. Anyway, you and I understand each other, we don't have to be like the man who wanted chicken for dinner.' I winked at her, she was staring at me. 'Is there anything wrong?'

'No, nothing, I was thinking about how much you men change with just a close shave and a warm shower. We, by contrast, require of elegant dresses, make up and an impeccable hairstyle to cause that same impression.' It was a compliment, discreet but direct; the conversation had raised to a higher level and I, for the first time in my life, was prepared.

'I think that you women underestimate yourself too much,' I said in a trusting tone. 'I know I don't have a very expressive face and that sometimes I don't find the opportune words, but I can tell you that you are the one to blame for for at least five minutes of my delay. Do you see that shadow at the entrance behind the column? There I was, hidden, undressing you with my eyes.'

She kissed me —please, reread the last phrase and take your time to recall your first kiss, your first real kiss. Now, resume the reading—. After that kiss we looked at each other and, as it couldn't be any other way, we understood each other. We ran out of the bar and, without slowing our pace, we covered the two blocks that separated us from the hotel; we went across the hall at full throttle and went upstairs, running up the stairs like two kids, up to my room. I know that describing sex scenes might seem somewhat gratuitous but I want to leave a faithful record of what took place that night in room 201, and not because that was my first time, which it wasn't, but because it was the first time different from the rest.

Well then, we entered the room and I kissed her, she undid my belt in return. I kept kissing her while she was whispering, what?, it didn't matter, a whisper is a whisper, something subtle and powerful. Without I noticing it she had taken my pants off and grabbed me with her hands delightfully cold; meantime I went on fondling the rear curve of her skirt. I turned her around of a sudden, grabbed her breasts with strength and went on lowering my hands down her body while biting her neck. And when all ten fingers slipped, and chanced upon the birthplace of her thighs, her thighs tensed up and pulled forward her teeny woman's belly; a drowned-out yell escaped from the well of her mouth. A propulsion engine ignited under the dark blue of her skirt, I felt its warmth. Little did I wait to lift it up and engage in careful caressing. I still had not seen her knickers but by the touch of them I could feel they were a modest pair, as those worn by women who still think themselves little girls. These were soft, she made them slid with her buttocks against my groin, turning her head from time to time, to kiss me or offer me a moan of hers on the very rim of my ear. She was gone, ¡we! were gone, up in flames… Kisses became wet, her mouth also. We got rid of the skirt, which in a blink had become such an unbearable nuisance, and at last I got to see the colour white of her basic underwear; white, the colour of in-nocence I thought, while I stripped it off and brought it to my mouth. Then I ventured in, went into a trance, she set her whispers aside and yelled loud. I wanted to devour her. With my hands, with my mouth… I could not help but look at her body for new flesh and shapes, in that same room where barely a few hours ago I had tickled ideas one shouldn't tickle ever. I had slipped again on wet tiles, I thought, I kissed her softly and went to sit on the chair by the desk. Her naked silhouette stood up from the bed and slowly tiptoed her way over, she sat on me. And when she began swinging her hips —her face two short millimetres from mine— we both lost control and began to make love.

Eventually, morning arrived and found us awake, naked in each other's arms. She turned around and looked at me. We were silent, discovering our faces under the newborn light. I was impatient to travel the world in quest for answers, and in two morning minutes, the time a flower takes to bloom, I realised everything I ever wanted to know was to be found in her eyes… green, nearly grey.

Second Part

I

I woke up disoriented, more than usual. But with a wide smile this time, instead of a gloomy face. And I would have slept the whole day (to be nearly three days awake is no small thing), but when the chambermaid knocked on the door I joyfully leapt up, naked as I was, and when I went to take the first step towards the door, she had already opened it and covered her eyes.

'I'm very sorry, sir,' she said, hiding her eyes behind her right hand, 'it's already time to check out, I thought the room would be empty.'

I kept walking straight to her with all my nonchalance hanging out and kissed her on the lips. Right after a 'What a wonderful day!' escaped my mouth, and I went into the shower. I don't know what was the maid's reaction, but I don't think she was displeased, at least now she would have a story to tell her colleagues during her break.

When I turned off the tap, after finishing my repertoire of catchy-crappy shower songs, the bathroom was full of steam, as if I were in a cloud, which was a good metaphor in fact to describe how I felt. However, the distorted image reflected in the steamed mirror reminded me of how lost I was. I brushed my teeth, rinsed my mouth, but I didn't manage to wash out the bitterness. I experienced a light comedown and lay down on the bed. There, stretched out and with nothing to do, I tried to think back… I believed recalling that the girl had left three hours ago (at that moment it was ten o'clock) to work, that I had offered to walk her to the Gallery and that she had said that I didn't have to, that I should better keep sleeping; and so I did. I couldn't recall anything else, I was really tired. And, of a sudden, a roar coming out from my stomach… I got dressed quickly and ran down to the restaurant before breakfast was over. The truth is I had a small stomach that wasn't used to copious meals, but it was a Saturday morning and I hadn't had a bite since Thursday's dinner; I guess my voracious appetite was more than justified. I wolfed down three fried eggs, three slices of fresh bread with assorted cheeses and cold cuts, three generously buttered pieces of toast with blueberry jam, a French almond croissant, a dark chocolate swirl bun, two cups of filter coffee and a good litre of orange juice.

And with my batteries fully charged, I was then ready to go out in search of my mysterious girl. I left the restaurant and crossed the hall more satisfied than a penguin when, just about to go out, I was called from reception:

'Excuse me, sir,' said the young receptionist and waited for me to approach the desk.

'What's the matter? I was just about to leave, I don't care about the receipt if that's…'

'Sir, you forget you owe the hotel the price of one night.'

'Nonsense, yesterday I paid before going up to my room.'

'You paid the price of one night, sir, which means there's still one night left to pay to close the bill.'

'Is it because I'm leaving one hour after my supposed checking out time?'

'Oh, no, sir. We haven't taken that into account. But…' he seemed to realise what was going on, 'Do you know it's Sunday, right?' My face of disconcertion talked in my place, 'I'm sorry sir, I will explain it to you: Yesterday morning a nice lady who said had spent the night with you which, by the way, we haven't taken into account either, told us that you wished not to be disturbed and, that if you hadn't gone down to have breakfast, it was because you wanted to stay another night with us.

'What!'

I paused for a few seconds to process what had just happened: it seems I had slept more than a whole day, nearly 27 hours —almost nothing—, and the hotel was going to charge me an extra night, a night worth 400 pounds, 500 euros… And while numbers were flying round and round over my head, like those little birds do in cartoons when a character receives a slap, I passed from astonishment to indignation on realising my flight to LA had taken off one hour ago, a flight that was worth… that was worth… —luckily for me nobody ever dies in cartoons, at least not from a heart attack, because very close was my heart to jumping out of my chest—. And so, overwhelmed by the numbers and the loss of time, with my pulse accelerated, I snapped: set my English manners aside, and started to vociferate and ask for explanations.

'So if anybody comes and tells you that whatshisname of room X wants to extend his stay, you simply put it through the computer without even consulting with whatshisname, not even to confirm the booking, and then you expect that whatshisname will take charge of the bill. Am I wrong?' When I realised I was speaking in Spanish I had already said everything.

'Sir, could you please lower your voice?' He replied, instead of asking me if I could repeat it in English for him, more attentive to appearance, bloody appearance!, than to my arguments; which drove me even madder.

'I could not,' I answered, and I repeated it all again, louder and with my back towards my interlocutor facing the hall, so every guest in the hotel could hear me, 'I could not!'

That guy must have been about my age but he was, in spite of his uniform, more of an adult size kid. His gaze betrayed him, as it betrayed the vast majority; his face, but his eyes above all, was of one who has never put anything into question or, at least, nothing worthwhile questioning; and what can I say about his cheeks, blushed out of the embarrassment I was pushing him to go through. He said nothing more, although I must say he never had a chance to add anything. The door behind the desk opened and the silhouette of a man leaned out for a few seconds, the enough to allow him, in an imperative and courteous tone, to invite me to what seemed to be his office. The timbre of his voice advised me to be cautious, so I forgot about the kid, who was now breathing relieved, and went in with the same indignation but with a different spirit, intimidated in a way. After crossing the threshold of his office I could see him better, his mature closely-shaved face showed off dignified wrinkles that, as the grey hair among the dark, gave him airs of distinction rather than airs of old age. Spruced up in a dark suit, he was sitting in a brown leather armchair, with his back upright and his arm extended inviting me to take a seat. His mere presence instilled authority, an authority that was mostly coming from his high-end glasses and their classic frame, which gave seriousness to a gaze that was already penetrating in itself. So I sat down. And in so doing everything got arranged in my head, I felt intuition flowing back and paid attention to it piously. I was being stingy, and if there was something that I did detest it was the stinginess of spirit, coming to hate it when this was manifested in me. And now, as an afterthought, wasn't that perhaps the motive of my departing? I talked first:

'My apologies for what happened…' I was about to explain myself, though it were just in broad terms, but in the end I refused to do it, tired of twenty years of vain words. 'Here you are, the four hundred pounds,' and put them on the majestic walnut desk.

'Is it true you slept an entire day?'

'And three hours more,' I answered.

'Whatever you've been through this week, it must have agitated you a great deal in order to put you into such a long sleep…' I liked how the word "agitated" sounded in his voice. I noted it in my mind.

Then he just paused, which made me think he was asking me for an explanation, but when I went to offer it he smoothly lifted the palm of his hand from the table, indicating that he hadn't quite finished yet, that he was just taking his time to find the most convenient words. He leaned forward a few centimetres, and when he opened his mouth he shut it again. He softened his countenance, relaxed his gaze. I knew immediately by his look that, just as I did, he had also opted to put the wherefores aside and give away his bare conclusion.

'Two hundred for me, two hundred for you,' he said while reaching over the table to take his part. 'Both parties contributed to the misunderstanding after all.'

He stood up. I stood up. A handshake followed. He instilled authority, an authority that was fair: the hotel should have been more formal, but I had spent two nights in it, one of them accompanied; I was to accept part of the blame. Besides, in my circumstances, I wasn't interested in drawing attention to myself. He kindly walked me to the hall and bid me farewell, reminding me that I would be welcome if I ever decided to stay there again.

In a certain way we were accomplices. Ignoring the image we were projecting one on the other, we had both seen ourselves reflected in our fellow man. Yes, I think it's right to say we were accomplices, accomplices in a curious situation: actors pushed to the stage, forced to improvise a script without rhythm, bereft of rhyme, laconic, of pats on the back and looks of complicity; a true script, of the kind that finds its way under the spectator's skin.

I left the hotel bewildered, as though I had just been bestowed the tools to understand a truth right on the brink of being revealed.

II

The wind was blowing out in the street, the air had cooled down and the wandering clouds in the sky were drifting together suspiciously. Anyway, there London extended before me, somewhat cooler and greyer than my dreamed California but still, all things considered, I was in London just as much of a stranger as I would have been anywhere else. Perhaps this was meant to be my destination, why not?

If life sends you to Japan and on the way you stumble into China, go into its temples and pray to an unknown God, fall in love with the local women or get lost: in its high mountains, in its stone forests, in its vast cities; go after millenary dragons and find them! Why not? That might as well be the real reason of our departure, always subtle and discreet as life itself, talking to us while hiding its face behind a newspaper of a day still to come.

I laughed to myself when I remembered the source of inspiration of what I had just written. Seven years had passed since my first trip to London, seven years since that incident my family and I had with the hotel reservation. When we arrived there the hotel turned out to be overbooked, and they redirected us to a sister hotel that was further away from the city centre. I was tired after the flight, but my father insisted and made our guide translate his words for the receptionist of the hotel in question. The conversation wasn't bearing the fruits that my father had expected and its tone became increasingly heated till the receptionist said, pointing to both hotels on the map, that they were not far apart enough to justify all that fuss. To which my father replied, out from the depths of his being, and also pointing to both hotels on the map, 'What do you mean no? This is as if I want to go to China and they take me to Japan!' Our guide didn't translate that sentence, and the receptionist, astounded, when he saw that my father was expecting a reply he asked about the two single words he managed to grasp, 'China, Japan?' Then I began to laugh at the absurdity of the situation and my mother, also laughing, convinced my father to let it go. Definitely that laughter lightened the mood, but my father didn't manage to raise a smile till the next morning when he saw the breakfast buffet. My father and I were very much alike in this sense, food would calm us down; whether to eat it, cook it or simply look at it. One week in London: the London Eye, Madame Tussauds, the Natural History Museum, long walks through the city, good restaurants, shopping days… and that is the scene whose memory I appreciate the most and thus the one I remember the best. I've always been amazed by the apparent randomness with which our brain stores our memories. We can entirely forget the day when a girl kissed us for the first time, even forget her name, forget that which caused us great disdain or boundless joy, and yet remember what we ate ten years ago for Christmas or a paragraph we memorised for some exam in high school. To dream about Venus and her exuberant sexuality, and upon waking up to misplace her body and her face and, yet, to firmly sustain the red bricks which once walled the grimy brothel where we found her…

Such were the thoughts flowing through while I was walking just to walk, and two thoughts further southwards I came upon the Thames. I stopped to contemplate with both arms on the riverside railing, the water was running dirty. However, I will say in its defence that its opaque green colour agreed with its nature; it could definitely not be of any other colour. Like when we see a man dressed as a woman and we notice there is something that doesn't quite fit, to imagine that same river wearing the crystalline waters of Majorcan coves was evoking an image that, more than daring, came across as indecorous, out of place.

Surroundings can be demolishing when they are not the propitious ones: cars will sink when trying to cross the ocean, seeds will die of thirst in the sandy soil and words will wither if not uttered at the right time. Cars need roads; moist soil, the seeds; and words, context.

Well, this is what my story was about, a poor individual going off the rails in search of his persona, of his place in the world. And now, at last, I had reasons to be optimistic, for I really felt as if I had reached my destination. I had missed my flight, yet the feeling was of arrival, as if the London where I had just disembarked was the sunniest and most colourful California. Which, upon second thoughts, made sense. I had always enjoyed the cold: going out for a run in short sleeves on winter nights and to feel how the gelid air would swell my lungs, tauten my skin and cleanse my mind. The first gasp of air before launching my legs into motion was an absolute ecstasy. But it was not only about the cold per se, but also about the kind of life to which the cold was preluding, a life of long nights, scarves, gloves and thick coats. It was, or at least it seemed to me, a propitious environment for introspection and good ideas. And at that moment, more than ever, I was in need of those good ideas to well up and undo the knots in my head. Damned be the day I fell entangled into the net!

The river was following its course... Silence came out of the blue, as out of the blue the flowing water froze. The traffic disappeared, in fact everything vanished except for the canvas I had right in front of me: white gusts of wind and of paint on top of other coloured but weaker gusts were covering it completely, just like a Pollock. However, in the upper right corner there were neither splatters nor drips, instead some meticulous brush-strokes could be appreciated illustrating, in the distance, a young couple gliding smoothly on the ice. At a glance one could see they were in love, and it wasn't because they were standing out with a brighter light —which they weren't—, but because they simply were there in their totality. No music was heard and they were moving so little they seemed to stand still; nevertheless no one could deny they were dancing. I took pleasure in looking at them and kept doing so till I saw myself attracted by a strange force. And *puff*, the distance between both observer and observed evaporated as if it had never existed. Now I found myself within that strange body in which I recognised, strangely enough, my pianist's hands and the tip of my Roman nose. Anyhow, in that moment, I wasn't questioning my being, I was simply conscious of my arms surrounding her waist, of hers surrounding my neck, the surface of the ice under our feet and the snowflakes falling on her reddish curls, which in turn were falling on her black dress. In the corners the young and the not-so-young were throwing snowballs at each other, and in the centre there were people skating about. Everything was idyllic, until a pair of eyes burning on my back broke the spell. I turned towards the railing, there was no one there. The ice creaked under our feet and the river melted away just as it had frozen. My body plunged into the water completely and, *puff*, I came back to my senses: dry, standing on solid ground and leaning on the railing.

With my feet in London, my eyes engaged in chimeras and utopias and my mind scattered everywhere it is no wonder I wasn't seen by that man, who was me and was not me, so dispersed was I across the four dimensions that comprise our universe…

The fragments of a point are not smaller points, the fragments of a point are nothing, fragmented people either.
Beings need to be —I concluded.

Invisible and fragmented, abstracted by the river's green flow, my mind slid into the green, nearly grey eyes that lit the night of my arrival. It felt good to remember, and I kept doing so with my notebook and pen in my hands when, of a sudden, I was lunged at from the right side, proving conclusively my incapacity to reflect light. I fell to the ground and when I opened my eyes my notebook was not there. I leapt up, terrified by the idea I had lost my most precious good, and right away I saw it at the edge, separated from the plunge by the most delicate equilibrium. I ran towards the notebook and grabbed it firmly. When I turned around I saw how my attacker was running away, without any apology whatsoever, trying in despair, shouting and waving, to catch the attention of a cab which he had definitely already missed. He shouted "joder" —the Spanish "fuck"— pissed off and many times while shaking his right fist at the sky. His helplessness soothed the blows of my fall and I considered myself avenged, so starving was I for a victory… For if it was indeed true that my head was constantly generating arguments trying to convince me that that was the place to be, so it was too that those were nothing more than a desperate attempt. Those weak arguments, like the thin layer of ice from my vision, were creaking and abandoning me to the wettest and coldest of all despairs under the pressure of the most insignificant hint of doubt.

Yes, I was in London, some ten hundred miles away from home, at last alone, and now what?

III

And now what? Visit museums? Walk around looking down with my hands in my pockets? Pretend to be amazed by every brick of this city? Take notes of my insignificant thoughts? Go back home? God, no! No way. That would be as though I had jumped up only because I knew with certainty my feet would land right on the same spot. I didn't see myself capable to bear it, to think of it was enough to sadden me to the bone. In doing so I would be making a false person of myself, a person that claims to be idealist and romantic but whose actions fall away from the idealism that he himself predicates. To take a step back in search of a shelter from the utopian vision prowling in front of me couldn't be a solution. It just couldn't.

It was the start of a headache. It became obvious to me that if I were to spend the whole day alone my own presence would amount to something unbearable, so I doubled back through Northumberland Avenue, towards Trafalgar Square, where I was hoping I would come across my anonymous lover. And right after passing by my hotel, we met head-on. I couldn't help smiling when I saw her, she was very pretty. The sunlight, filtered by the clouds, was falling on her, gently on her blonde and long hair, much blonder and much, much longer than what I recalled; falling on her white silken skin, on her face perfectly drawn, on the smile she raised when she saw me…

When we moved closer together and found ourselves standing up one right in front of the other, neither of us knew in which manner we should greet. Should we shake hands? A kiss on the cheek, or one on the lips? And what about a hug? At the end our greeting ended up being a kiss-hand-hug mix in its clumsiest version. We had slept together, but it was evident we were still strangers to one another and neither of us seemed to know how to act. The atmosphere smelled of confusion, of shyness and of carnations in wintertime.

It was I who spoke first and, as every other fool in love with slow wit, I began to talk about the weather:

'It seems it's going to rain,' with my hands inside my pockets and signalling the sky with my head.

'Yes…' as if sighing, 'I brought a jacket,' signalling the one she was wearing, a thin cardigan with unequal horizontal lines of different shades of brown; it suited her very well on top of her loose-fitting white t-shirt, 'because it began to cool down but I should have brought an umbrella instead. Maybe both. Here in London sometimes it cools down or begins to pour all of a sudden, sometimes both at the same time. The weather is abrupt,' she said in a shy manner, although with her particular spontaneity. After a few seconds of the most pleasant uncomfortable silence, it was she who spoke, 'Shall we walk?'

And as if movement had brightened us up, after a few steps we found ourselves walking arm in arm. We were strangers indeed, but strangers willing to get to know each other better.

We came across the river again at the end of the street.

'Have you ever been on the London Eye?' She asked, pointing at the giant wheel that was spinning at the other side of the river.

'Yes, I have. When I came with my family seven years ago. I think it was what we enjoyed the most in London.'

'I've also been on it a few times, I love it. The first time I went it was also with my parents, they took me on the same day it opened, about ten years ago. I was just a girl back then and it really impressed me. Totally worth the long queue. It was a very nice family day.'

'Do you still live with your parents?' it occurred to me to ask.

She smiled in a strange way, with her lips closed, the commissures slightly raised, while her eyes, whose expression completely escaped my comprehension, were aimed sideways at me. Her smile didn't manifest sadness nor joy, neither seemed its reason to lie between both feelings. In a strange way, how Mona Lisa smiled to Leonardo Da Vinci five hundred years ago.

'Would you like to go for a ride?' She said, changing the topic without bothering to dissimulate.

'Well, yes, why not?' I clumsily replied.

We decided to cross the river via one of the Golden Jubilee Bridges, a pedestrian bridge that —according to her— shared the foundations of the Hungerford Railway Bridge and which just happened to be less than ten metres on our right. When we had already walked across half of the bridge I couldn't help asking:

'Has the Thames ever frozen?'

'Yes, of course, why are you asking?'

'I was just thinking it would be a nice image, I would like to see it.'

'That's going to be difficult, as far as I know it has not frozen since 1814, at least in the London metropolitan area.'

'Wow, this is what I call precision!'

'Don't be amazed, it's just that, last year at the National Gallery, we exhibited posters and paintings that depicted the fairs they used to have on the tideway when it froze, as well as some souvenirs, commemorative cards and other artefacts that used to be sold there. And, if memory serves me right, 1814 was the year when the last frost fair took place. Afterwards, in 1831, the Old London Bridge was demolished, already obsolete, and the new one with fewer and wider arches was inaugurated, so helping the tide to flow more freely. That's why, no matter how cold it's been in subsequent years, it has never frozen again. Actually, there have been some years in which a thin layer of ice has formed on the surface, but nothing more.'

'With seeing this thin layer of ice I would be content.'

'Yes, me too, I've never seen it.'

And without noticing we had already bought our tickets, twenty pounds each, and were getting ready to go into one of those glass pods of the wheel, the two alone. Thereinto the world was another:

'If it were cheaper I would probably come more often. Or not, I think I would just ride in it just about the same number of times, once or twice a year,' she said, correcting herself. 'Going into one of these revolving cabins is the closest thing I know to escaping this world. Were I to incorporate it to my daily life, I assume it would lose a large part of its charm.'

'I don't think I would ever get tired of it,' I said, gaping at the sights and bewitched by the breathable peace in there.

'Yes, you would,' she replied, confident of what she was saying.

She was sitting on the wooden bench at the centre of the pod and I was on my feet looking at the view and moving around to and fro, faithfully committed to my role as a tourist. When our pod reached the peak of the wheel, she approached me from behind my back and kissed my cheek unexpectedly. I kissed her back on her lips, a soft and tender kiss. A spark had crackled and we were getting ready to smooch in the intimacy of the world's outskirts when, my lips already brushing hers, she began to speak cheerfully:

'I forgot! The Thames also froze in the great freeze of 1963. I'm sorry,' she said when seeing my face startled, 'it's just that I was brooding on it because I remembered we also exhibited photographs that showed the Thames completely frozen and thought it was impossible those photographs had been taken back then. I don't even think any kind of camera had been invented before 1830.'

She was just like that and it was impossible not to desire her. In that moment I didn't even remember the missed flight to California, as if it had never been relevant, as if nothing else had ever mattered to me but to be there with her.

IV

After a thirty minute ride in the London Eye we decided to go for a drink. We walked past a few pubs but she didn't stop at any of them, she seemed to have a specific place in mind. Again we crossed the river, but via Westminster Bridge this time; the most famous London icon, Big Ben, towered at the end of the bridge. But I didn't pay much heed to the emblematic watch, I had taken her by her hand and was worried mine would sweat too much. My gait was distracted. We turned two or three corners and finally went into a pub of intimate atmosphere: with dim lights, a prominent bar and sofas built into the wall. Subdued colours predominated in there, and the colour of dark wood. There were people, but not too many. We sat at the bar and right afterward the barman came over.

'A lemonade,' she asked.

'A Coca-Cola,' it was the ideal place to have a beer but at that moment I didn't fancy alcohol, so I breathed relieved when I saw she didn't want to drink alcohol either.

'Is Pepsi ok?' asked the waiter amiably while polishing a beer glass with a cloth.

'Yes, Pepsi's fine. Excuse me, could it be light?' I asked the waiter when he had already taken two steps towards the fridge.

'No problem at all, sir.'

When I turned back to her she was looking at me.

'What?' I asked.

'Nothing,' translation: I found your little scene with the waiter amusing.

He served us and we drank half of our soft drinks in one go, silence fell between us once more. Though it did disappear quickly when she took, out from the inner pocket of her jacket, a small white notebook.

'Look,' she said while handing me her notebook.

'*Sentences with no sense*,' read the title she had written on the cover; I was surprised by her handwriting, incredibly similar to mine, like the one you could imagine in a passionate letter written in fountain pen. I opened the notebook and began to leaf through it with curiosity before she could say anything; it was overflowing with letters and words.

'From here the man who wanted chicken for dinner. Nobody had ever shown as much interest in one of my sentences as you did and I thought you might like to hear a few more,' she looked a little insecure at that moment, as though she feared being tiresome with her oddities by which, on the contrary, I was rather charmed.

'And you're right. Let's see what we have here…' I went back to the first page and read the first sentence, *'What for does the dog that does not bark pull the chain?'* I was flabbergasted, she laughed at the face I made. I read another one, *'Why do stones allow trees to yawn?'* And another, *'But if the blue bird overtakes the blue bear, would that mean that the green ostrich is a brown pig?'* My face was smiling, those sentences were wonderfully absurd. She was quiet, making an effort to contain her laughter. I read another, this one more mathematical, *'If $1+1=3$ and $2+2=-14$, $7+7=?$* Am I supposed to answer? All the sentences are questions,' she laughed loudly.

'No, no,' she replied when she eventually got her breath back. 'I simply began with a question and kept writing more questions. There's no reason behind it, although if I had to guess I would simply say that it is difficult to change certain patterns once you get them started. Have a look at the next page.'

'Let's see… *Why do apples fall down and pears sing?* You see, another question! Wait, that one is not: *I would have apple stuffed with pear for breakfast if it were ten o'clock at night in Tokyoland.* What the hell? Where did that come from?' Laughs, laughs and more laughs; I read more and more, enough so as to think they would soon stop being funny and, in fact, laughter did dwindle away, but they certainly did not bore us for each sentence I read was more extravagant than the last, '*Wait for a frog, soon it will rain.* Yeah, it does seem is gonna rain, but I'm not waiting for no frog,' I know that my comment was absurder and sillier than her sentence but I could not contain myself. '*Necessity is a duck*,' this last one intrigued me a great deal, just as the one about the man who wanted chicken for dinner had done, so I inquired, 'Does this sentence have any story behind?'

'It is a good one, isn't it? It is one of my favourites, short, simple and intriguing. I'm sorry to tell you, though, I don't have any story for this sentence, it just popped up in my mind and I wrote it down.'

'I don't believe you. Is it about a hunter?' She laughed again.

'There's no story this time, seriously.'

'That's a shame.'

'Not necessarily. I'll tell you what, I'll leave this one to you, you are in charge this time. I just expect you'll let me know if you find any kind of meaning or sense in it, deal?'

'Deal,' I replied. Although I didn't intend to take it seriously, I already had too many things in my head.

We took another large gulp of our virgin drinks.

'Do you know what's curious about it?' She asked; I didn't know what she was referring to.

'What?'

'That even though I call them sentences with no sense, every single one of them has something of me in it, and even though I'm not always able to see their sense I'm convinced they all carry one.'

'And precisely *Necessity is a duck* is one of those sentences abandoned of all reason, eh?' I insisted.

'Yes, you have fallen for a difficult sentence. But remember, *Don't be like the man who wanted chicken for dinner* was of the same kind and at the end its story came out.'

'I know, but from your head, following its composition.'

'And that very moment when I composed it, as you say, some three years ago now —so you get an idea for how long I've been doing this— was the conception of our first night together.'

'First? So perhaps there will be another one?' I should have paid more attention to what she had just said, but I suppose that my libido was somewhat higher than usual at the time.

'Maybe…' she answered mischievously. 'Anyway, now you try it, try to make up a sentence with no sense, you'll see how I deconstruct it.'

'Ok, ok, just give me a second…' I tried to think but not a single word would come to my mind. She was waiting and I was getting nervous as the seconds went by; the nerves of one who knows he is going to be evaluated. Not knowing what to expect, I made the decision to exhale and move my lips and tongue randomly and see what would come out:

> 'Two cans, one of Pepsi, one of Fanta.
> The ship is falling, the plane is sinking.
> The sea is green, but it is not an ad for 7-UP,
> rather a submerged forest
> who fearful of fire sank.'

'Wow! That's what I call depth! Are you a poet? In any case, do you see now how difficult it is to do something with no sense?'
'What do you mean?'
'This poem talks about you, look: it's evident you mentioned the drinks inspired by those we have right here,' she said pointing to the cans, already empty. 'The ship and the plane might be machines that had a lot of influence on your life, you are smart, there is no doubt about it, you might have studied something related to them, aircraft or nautical engineering; besides, the most logical phrasing would have been to say that the one which is falling is the plane and the one which is sinking is the boat, the alteration in

the word order suggests a complex personality, also the fact you used the verbs to fall and to sink tells me you are in trouble, maybe with your studies. When it comes to the green sea, as you mentioned it along with the word 'ad', I think that the sea is more about your appearance than about your actual being and I know this because you spoke later about a forest that submerges itself underwater and drowns due to its fear of getting burnt.' She paused, I was stupefied. 'You are the forest! That's it! You are the forest and the sea is your appearance which is choking you, and you allow it because you believe that, otherwise, to breathe and live could kill you.' I was downhearted, but the face of my downheartedness only made her speak up more, 'You know it, you do know it! That's why you are hungry and don't want to eat,' pointing to my thin complexion, 'that's why you are sleepy and don't want to sleep,' pointing to the bags under my eyes, 'you are living, you are just not used to it, that's all. I know it might seem absurd but it is not absurd if it really is true.'

Annoyed by the string of undercover truths that with so gracious a violence she had aired, I got angry with her and left without giving her a chance to utter a single word more. I left the bar, with my erection cast down, and walked aimlessly, looking at the ground, overwhelmed by all those thoughts I believed I had left behind.

The unstable feelings had been agitated. My steps sped up, my hands clenched, the eyes reddened. A hard rain came out of nowhere, as a pathetic fallacy, affine to my tears of rage. I ran amongst black umbrellas and inquisitive glances judging me as I brushed past them. I wasn't too conscious of my surroundings, I knocked down an old woman and was nearly ran over when crossing the street; in both cases I kept running and kept my hurried pace until I found myself alone in one of those green parks of the city; St. James Park read the sign. The hard rain was now barely a weak drizzle. The grey clouds contrasted with the wet grass. The green was dense. I took two more steps to sit down on the wooden bench. There, seated, I was staring at how the thin drops were pattering on the lake and were making it tremble delicately. Their effect was hypnotic…

V

There, seated, alone on that bench, I was drawn to think about what she had said before I ran off from the bar: '…that's why you are sleepy and don't want to sleep…'. For nearly four years I had been blaming my few and fewer hours of sleep on a chronic insomnia but then, after listening to her, I thought insomnia might not be what was ailing me, perhaps it wasn't even an ailment at all. Insomnia is suffered by those who, wanting to sleep, can't manage it, but the truth is that I didn't have any desire to sleep. To dream…, now that was something else. But to sleep…, well, at least not early, because I recognise that once within that peace, on the margins of the world and time, I could lie in that state for more than twelve hours. Even entire days, as I've recently seen for myself. However, the alarm clock has always been a constant in my life. Oh, yes, there has not been in my life a more annoying object, because although it was true that I could sleep for more than twelve hours, so it is that very few times have I been able to get far enough from the world and time so as not to hear the rays of morning sunlight pounding on the window pane. Morning roared in the noisy traffic, in the shouts of my mother complaining about my attachment to my pillow, in the bells that are and the chimes of those yet to be invented. In the chalks cast by cantankerous teachers! Go where I might its inopportune presence was embodied in one of its demoniacal representatives, always drumming and clattering when the sweetest honey was to fall on my lips, at two nanoseconds from a dream about to climax. But enough! I have had enough. No more turning the alarm off and begging the morning to delay five more minutes the day. To eat whenever hungry and to sleep whenever feeling like it. Forget about poetic definitions, this is the true freedom!

Not long ago I saw a film on one of those nights in which I was shunning sleep. There are films that, at their ends, leave you wondering whether everything lived by the protagonist were not a mere product of his imagination; but this one in particular went further. When my morning arrived, already late afternoon, I didn't know whether I had actually dreamed the whole film, because it really seemed to have come from there, the world of dreams. This effect was to do with the unusual story, the extravagant characters, the strange scenes that seemed not to fit with the rest yet somehow blend in finely; and, above all, the Italian melody with which it was narrated, a melody that the Castilian-speaker understands in the same way he recognises the lights and shadows of the dreams he's able to remember. I've never enjoyed subtitles, but I must admit that had I not seen it in its original version, it would have lost great part of its magic. Italian, the language of dreams. That night it earned the title.

Dark eyes, what a beautiful film! Its protagonist, Romano, as a child would cover his ears so as not to hear the lullaby his mother sang. He was convinced that as soon as he fell asleep the best part of the night would ensue, that he would miss the most beautiful things that could take place. That's why I say it is not insomnia, but rather the will to not sleep. But call it what we might, we could say that that wakefulness induces us to a dream of open eyelids, a dream that brings us closer to death, stripping off our perception of reality, attracting monsters a sane mind would repel! And even then there it is, inspiration, in that trance that is not a trance, a thin blind of illusion, barely tangible, on which for a moment we believe to see projected our hidden yearnings, truths that in our dreams talk, that aspire to be understood whilst expressing themselves clumsily with ineffable symbols only visible to the tired mind which, being awake, longs to dream.

Meditating about insomnia, ironically, I yawned. It is said that the more one sleeps, the more one feels like sleeping; people say a lot of things, but in this case they seemed to be right. I felt the impulse to take my notebook out from the inner pocket of my jacket and I didn't repress myself.

Dreamer, do not fall asleep, please do scrawl intelligibly your somnambulist pen-strokes.

How much I would have liked at that moment to discover she had run after me, I really was wishing to tell my story to someone. I waited a few minutes more, giving her some extra time to appear behind me. But she didn't show up and I felt contradictorily relieved. Tears ceased, ceased the rain. The calm after the storm.

A blink, a pigeon's wing, and the dark eyes I had in mind materialised in the sockets of a young lady of mystic beauty. She appeared as if she had been there from the very beginning and I hadn't taken notice of her presence. She had a serious expression and her gaze fixed on me. She was about seven metres from the bench where I was sitting, steady, on her feet, close to the shore. Behind her, twenty-one ducks bathing on the lake. Her skin was white and her cheekbones, rosy. Her lips, red as the petal of a rose. Her hair, long like a fairytale princess', parted in the middle, was falling plentiful over one of her shoulders; it was orangey red and straight, on no account lank. She wore a long t-shirt or a short dress, with a pattern that alternated the colours green and fuchsia; on top of this she wore a long and unbuttoned knitted jacket and, underneath, a skirt that covered her legs and her feet. The jacket was navy blue tending towards black, the skirt was full dark. She seemed to be floating on the grass.

A blink, a pigeon's wing, and she vanished. She didn't belong to this world, didn't I belong to hers; not yet.

I yawned again seated on that wet, hard and uncomfortable bench…

VI

'Why?' said a deep and resounding voice, starting off the most twisted and perturbing dream I ever had the luck to plunge into.

I found myself in a rectangular room, built entirely with wood that was clearly unvarnished. The unbalanced benches on which I was sitting among other individuals, the floor perceptibly inclined towards the right rear corner, the nails protruding from it, the splinters… they all gave away the many competences of a sloppy carpenter. The walls of that sinister scenery were fully clothed with long worn out drapes, red and undulating, like the guardian curtain of a theatre in ruins and its secrets. And even though I soon noticed the ill-worked wood and the threadbare walls, it took me a little longer to notice the people of this eldritch world. As though they were downloading themselves from a remote unit, or were there just in part and were waiting for a trigger to materialise completely, they were blurry. There were even a few that seemed to be formed by the snow of a channel-less TV: black and white pixels in movement were shaping a human silhouette from whose stomach emerged the irksome noise of a milliard flies buzzing. Afterwards, I heard two hammer blows claiming my attention in front of me, where I could appreciate all the elements of a court of law. Then I recognised myself among the public and, as if those two hammer blows had been two benign blows on a TV, the blurry audience materialised completely. Of human proportions, strange beings, eunuch, white like nothingness, had no mouth nor nose, and were only wearing a bowler hat interwoven with their own hairs and a pair of sunglasses stuck to their own skin, as if both accessories were just another appendage of their uncomfortably lustrous body. I began to fret, the atmosphere was lugubrious, almost eerie, and the air smelled like sulphur and wouldn't let me breathe, it was smothering me while interfering thoughts, like stabbing crystals, were besieging my mind. I closed my eyes and yelled, yelled vehemently! Yells of pain, panic and anguish were freely grating out from my insides when, of a sudden, two ponderous syllables thundered all over the room. When I opened my eyes I was calmed and serene, seated where only the defendant should sit. I seemed to be the only responsible for a crime that hadn't yet been revealed and, as such, from my privilegedly condemnatory position, the first thing I saw was a fresh and loathsome stain oozing down, with its mustard colour, on the smart yet minute black gown of a pig-faced dwarf judge. Instead of a bench an imperial armchair raised the judge high enough to compensate his short stature, and I was, so it seemed, to explain myself before him and the intimidating whitish beings.

As every dream does, this one had an odd and not too convincing atmosphere; or so I'm saying now that I'm awake, because at that very moment I could feel the vibration of my vocal chords when talking, the touch of the unvarnished wood, the pain in my eyes when looking at the ochre stain on the judge's gown and a sickly smell evoking the iodine whiff of hospitals. And all that made me feel that, were they to have me beheaded in that dream, there would be no awakening able to put my head back on its place. I also had to say that it was hot, very hot, as if the red drapes that enclosed the scene were the very same flames of hell. Then I remembered who were that received the greatest punishment in the scorching caverns of the netherworld: the cowards, the indifferent, the ones scared of death and of living life. I decided to face that fear, and not out of bravery or fear of something worse, but because bitter death is not that bitter if the life that it takes is a life that is sour. And I, not knowing why, was suffering in that moment, suffered so much I was convinced death would be a sweet morsel. "Well," said Mr Sammler in Saul Bellow's brilliant novel, "people went to wars. They took what weapons they had, and they advanced toward the front." So I stood up and positioned myself instinctively where I could better be heard. I was the accused in a demonic trial, a situation as terrifying as absurd, and before deciding whether I had to take it seriously or as a joke, I began to talk without any objective nor full control over my words:

'My gaze has grown cold after reflections of atrocious images, and tired after the endless recreation of these in my dreams, which once used to be my only means of escape. It might be that the accumulation of those lived experiences, combined with an imaginative mind and a chaotic memory, contributed to the creation of those nightmares which I, already used to them, can familiarly address as mere dreams…

'My lungs open up when I smell the scent of red roses in that beautiful and cursed rose-field, despite having checked their petals were in truth white and their smell was indeed that of blood. My legs do not step any measurable length back, by no means is my face horrified, when feeling on my chest the acute pain of an ownerless sword mercilessly thrusting back and forth from the blackest shadow.

'Do not misinterpret me, my sorrow is not having been born but having lived enough so as to contemplate evil and recognise it in my reflection, as to hear the cries of pain, help and regret of all those who, conscientious or not, represented it as either a victim or a criminal, when I found myself alone and in silence.

'You will think that with this speech I'm just giving you more reasons to sentence me, miserable hypocrites, and it doesn't surprise me. I've pronounced words that made me fear and loathe my own presence. I will have made the most indecisive ones determined and turned my once faithful supporters against me. Anyone who might have heard my so inopportune words will have realised that my rotten mind cannot even invent a plausible lie pertinent to the given circumstances, which is what everyone was expecting. I don't care, I know that if I am here it is not because there were serious doubts cast on my version of the facts and I had now to prove my innocence; this trial is a mere formality, a stage on which it has already been decided I'm guilty. But I don't intend to take on my role, to feed with my plea the farce you've just created. This theatre, this pure fiction.

'Well, gentlemen, here is where I wanted to bring you all, because there is nothing in this world that is more real than fiction. (I know you've been listening to my divagations for quite some time and that with this last crazy affirmation you might be feeling like shutting me up, but I beg you to be patient). Fiction is not time machines, laser beams nor flying saucers.

Fiction is this deceitful life in which we are submerged, and it is real because we accept it and feel it as such, but that doesn't stop it from being a fallacy, an illusory image that occurs on the margin of truth. One must be capable of differentiating truth from deceit as one should distinguish from what is lived what is dreamed, otherwise one could become mad. But this nobody teaches us, not even are we alerted to the danger to which we are exposed and, although we are born without scratches, when growing we do so as though the surroundings were a mould and we the raw dough, adapting ourselves to it, learning to walk amid superstructures of ferrous knowledge. And in this way, with a prudent gait, step by step, a very particular vision of the world is spread and in an intolerant way generalised: cataloguing, studying and eradicating any perception falling off its lit field. BARBARITIES! ATROCITIES! DRIVELS! MONSTROSITIES! FOLLIES! FRIGHTS! HORRORS! In this world that holds us, reason seems to be motive enough to be in favour of whoever preaches it, and people give themselves piously to that cult of rationalism, without questioning its entangled arguments; at least not enough! Because a minimum of scepticism before what is seen and what is hidden, of conviction in what we do, of devotion to life, of promptitude to make our wishes come true, would make us ask ourselves whether everything that claims to be reason is indeed reason at all.

'But to you, gentlemen, we are only a handful of individuals, right? Right! And from so much repeating it to ourselves we've ingenuously come to believe it. Nevertheless, I'll tell you that who trusts and is after betrayed stops being an ingenuous. Now I own a deep voice and a cold gaze, a firm pulse and a determined mind; I can cry of happiness and laugh at my own misfortunes, so don't trouble yourselves in setting me a righteous example. I shall find righteous nothing!' I felt my hand was trembling; I took a deep breath and waited a few seconds before proceeding.

'I was in that place where life goes to die, a long time with my downcast gaze laid on the turbid water of a reflectionless swamp, and that place is never forgotten, it is remembered with esteem as we do with our most vivid sadnesses. Silence empired in that devastated land; lost souls wandering there were neither sobbing nor making noise when walking. I was sharing penitence as one more of them, but one day, as desolated as any other, *unkent* voices in my head asked: "Where do the ravings of sane people go if not to Oblivion?" I wanted to answer but didn't find any words, as he who retches and yet can't throw up. Then I felt a harrowing pain in my head, as if a worm were biting its way among the pleats of my grey matter. And when I was about to faint of torment the same voices answered: "They repress their ravings so fiercely in their mind they not get to hear them even once. And not being able to flow these remain in there, stagnant, withering with no air or movement, rotting up the mind that harbours them." I understood then, those worms were nothing but my ravings becoming aware of my dozing being. An agonising transition. For days I lay on those swampy lands writhing in pain. A piercing pain, of those that feed themselves gobbling down the cries of the person who suffers them. Needless to say, the pain ceased, but not without first breaking my muddied armour which didn't admit such a torsion. And there there was, underneath, my immaculate skin; there there was, behind the clouds, the Sun.

'Yes, "individual" is such an artificial term that can dehumanise whoever it addresses. And this dehumanisation is the one that brings to life the most perverse of all fictions, the one that clothes man and impedes us to see him as such, the one that corrects his language and educates our ears so we can't listen to his words as mere words. This is the dehumanisation that discredits men who like me decided to bring to light their clandestine habits and thus to ignore, despite not being printed in any leather-bound book, the established rules the whole world knew. Now I'm addressing those men and women, those men and women that decided to live as persons in a world of apparent individuals, and I say apparent because I reckon not everything is lost: remember that beneath that thick layer of identities and reaffirmations underlies sculpted our soul, pure, atemporal…

'What an irony! Humanity, determined to generalise diversity, has left those who comprehend her in dire straits; forcing them to accept their low condition as an individual, they must renounce their unique and irreplaceable persona just to confine themselves to be one more of society, a society that doesn't care about who you are, your fears, your character, your past, your concept of beauty, the way you comprehend air and feel the wind… your intensest hatred… Nothing it cares about us, and nevertheless it dares to judge us when we proclaim ourselves lords of our fate, because it turns out we do care about that bluebird that's in our heart —as Bukowski well expressed—, that sad and moribund singer that moans during the day and weeps with us at night.'

'Sir, you are here today for throwing a desk at who was once your teacher…' said the judge that didn't understand anything that was coming out of my mouth.

'Do you know what, sir? You remind me of my mother,' laughs in the courtroom, 'yes, my mother. You see, sir, I used to tell my mother about confusing thoughts and choked feelings in my throat. I told her about experiences I wanted to live, told her I wanted to be a writer and travel the world or, better still, get lost in it. She loved me, and a lot, I would even dare to say that she admired me in secret, that she understood my ideals and shared them. But she had to undertake the mother's role society expected from her, the same way her own mother had one day to put her feet on the ground, she had now to talk reason to me. However, truth doesn't listen to reason, it simply occurs, like the singular forms ice takes when melting. And the truth is that I left, that she is not here, that my world has widened. Why should my unbowed conscience shoulder regrets? There's no guilt to divide up; I, at least, don't see it. Time goes by and truth happens, no one can prevent it, no one should blame oneself for it.

'However you, all of you!' already shedding tears, 'Insist on silencing my voice, on censoring my thoughts, on pressuring me to repress my emotions, and now you dare to fine my acts! Well then, I tell you that we might bear love,' referring to men that still are men, 'face war; we might ask for forgiveness, feast on our hunger and drink down our thirst, we might even have our life taken and survive despite all. Call it epiphany, call it inspiration, call it life!, but that which grows and multiplies is capable of enduring anything merely for its own right to exist. And I'm so sure of my existence as I'm sure this is all a dream,' already aware of where I was, 'My dream! That's why I tell you: judge me!, sentence me to capital punishment if this is what you want. But I warn you, when breathing my last I'm going to awake, and then, it will be you who will die.

'Why? Because!' Shouted a powerful voice rising from my insides. 'Damn scumbags…' concluded the same voice, already out of breath.

You might find the following rather strange, but I could have sworn I made a small mistake of precision and died in my dream before waking up, for there was an extended moment in which everything went pitch dark and nothing but my thoughts could be perceived… That's why, when I woke up and opened my eyes, it was evident the world that appeared before me was but an extension of myself, as if the same light radiated by the sun were emerging straight from my eyes. Although, as I soon discovered when my eyes adapted to the glow and could finally see, there was no sun shining in that moment but a pair of spotlights instead. I got up from the floor and looked around, I found myself standing on an empty stage in front of an attentive audience. It was as if those specimens had turned into people, beings of common faces and expressive gestures, of distinctive features each handsomer than the last, able to smile, to procreate, able to take their hat off and look at the world without the need of having first to filter its glaring light. Somehow I felt it was me who had converted them, that thanks to me they were not simple individuals anymore.

Since I saw Charles Chaplin's *The Great Dictator* that I wished to do one, a soliloquy, improvise heartfelt words out loud and, like Chaplin, be understood, reach the soul of my listeners and be applauded at the end. This was my chance so, completely aware, and intuiting I was floundering on the surface of a shallow dream, I addressed them without hesitation:

'If this was a dream I wouldn't want to wake up. Although my sleeping body had to forever lie on swampy lands. In my search I discovered that the bottom of my black pupils is but the cornea of an even deeper sight, that the fateful mantle from which the stars are hanging is but the surface of a higher world… And at some point in this infinity I found some tense vocal chords and the air needed to make them vibrate. I lost my identity, abandoned my possessions, left home, renounced my name! But it was worth all the loss, now I can raise my voice and talk to you, tell you I've seen enough so as to say that seeing has no end, and when saying so be sure of it. Thank you, thank you very much for contemplating, from your higher world, the worldly experiences of this errant man who razed everything to find a voice and make it his.'

The audience stood up and applauded. The sensation was of gratitude and pride. Recognition.

VII

'My voice...' I murmured, still half asleep.

I finally opened my eyes, the clouds had disappeared and the sun reached its peak in the sky. My neck was killing me, for I had, as it seemed, had something more than a doze on that bench; had spent there the entire night. And that dream... All dreams are akin and at the same time they all differ, like people, but the one just dreamed was standing out from the rest, it kept being incoherent and confusing in delivering its message, alright, but it seemed to put a greater effort into its narration, as if saying: hey man, pay attention. And so I did. Even then I didn't get much clear from that chaotic-baroque discourse, but in a way, although I didn't get absolved from my sins, I had forgiven myself.

Just like in our eyes when slanted by a happy smile always a speck of dust or a thin and small broken vein can be glimpsed, the dark passages of our life are not as dark as we believe them to be. There are needles of light all along, occasional thick white rays even. Golden oblique floods of it. Red and orange heavy chunks. Quasi violet spears. This much light I discovered, at last, when venturing to look at the past with neither wrath nor resentment.

He was shy, he undervalued his voice before everyone else's, for which he forced himself to study in advance everything he had to do and say. His successful life had nurtured such behaviour, as to all appearances it was giving him good results. And so he grew up to be a cold and calculating subject, somewhat proud of his premeditated speech and unchanging temper, yes, but unwilling as well to face the demons that made him suffer more and more each day...

How curious the pattern that a line of ink draws when it is moistened by a tear... Curved and blurred, like a memory that fades. Because tears were back, but not like the ones I had shed before, these tears were composed and well-rested. It was like uncorking a good bottle of wine.

He seemed to go mad, pretending normality whilst his world was caving in. Pillars were collapsing, entire façades coming down. He came to think his fate was to wander about debris until death found him crushed under a wall or pierced by a rusty iron beam. He genuinely was sad, depressed, dispirited, lost, dispersed... like the dust that one day were a pretty porcelain vase of purple lavender and pink cyclamen.

Even then he kept walking, more out of the spinning momentum of his legs than out of strength and hope. And the wheel was slowing down, little by little was losing its balance, it was wobbling… And when it fell, and was mere dust among dust, it rose with a gentle puff of air.

That last sentence made me smile. From dust among dust to dust in air. Light, with no more weight than the memory of a past life and the wish to undertake the one lying ahead, I was floating away in the hope the breeze would lead me towards that imprecise dream of which I still knew so little. "A man is capable of going as far as his imagination reaches," I heard in a documentary I saw in secondary school about how the pyramids of Egypt were built. And I, despite not having felt it, believed, with the particular distrust of youth, that that sensation of freedom I was capable of imagining had to exist. When I would mention it to my parents (who would describe themselves realistic) they would just advise me to focus on my studies and brand me starry-eyed and, know what?, I might be a starry-eyed but, fuck, how good it feels to be one! I don't censor them, I understand their point of view, in the sense that I know the way they have of perceiving the world, not too different from the one I had before starting my studies, not too different from the one I had before starting this journey!, a world that is neither sad nor grey —warm and cosy even—, but which differs from my current vision, much more lively and glowing.

I remember having asked London to help me undo the knots in my head. Back then I thought I was asking too much, but there was no doubt at that point the city had thrown itself into its given task.

At the other side of the door I could hear the lock being manipulated: rig-rig, rig-rig, rig-tag... clicked, every time closer to finding the right combination.

Third Part

I

Still in St. James Park, the peaceful movement of the clouds was gently easing the pain in my neck, which didn't hurt that much anymore. There was a cloud that seemed a swan lying down, face up just as I was, staring at an even higher sky. This was spinning around its centre of gravity, deforming itself, and in a few seconds it evolved into a dragon spitting fire. I closed my eyes again, so calmed and serene I was. I didn't fall asleep but lay there stretched out for about an hour, half unconscious, until a football hit me in the face and woke me up fully. I have said it a few times already, this is one of the things that infuriates me the most, to be woken up with bad manners. I kicked the ball, as I used to when I was younger and played for my hometown team. The ball was headed towards the face of the first guy I saw who, inconveniently, happened to be the stockiest and who dodged it with surprisingly sharp reflexes. I soon reassessed the situation: myself being a foreigner, shooting a ball against a local surrounded by friends was not the best way to integrate oneself, but the best way to earn a beating. But England wouldn't stop surprising me, when seeing the power and precision of my shot —pure luck— they invited me to join in. I would have liked to accept, but I had other plans; plans that I was forced to postpone a few hours due to the wildest hunger I had ever felt, even wilder than the one I experienced the day before yesterday in the hotel during breakfast time. In my stomach a lion roared.

Can you guess what I ate? Roast chicken! Half, with copious amounts of mashed potatoes. In the first restaurant I found. Since Friday evening, when I heard her tell the story of the man who wanted chicken for dinner, that I had it clucking in my head. Eventually I satisfied my whim and sated my appetite, I was then ready to move on to the next thing: Trafalgar Square. With a vague idea of my exact location, I fumbled around towards it. I turned a few wrong corners so I had to go down long streets two and even three times, but I didn't mind it for I took the chance to stroll and do some sightseeing. If I'm honest, I think I was turning the wrong corners on purpose. Well, I don't think, I'm sure of it. A desire to walk, that is what I had, for when I stumbled upon the Big Ben I was already orientated and, even then, I decided to cross the Thames along the neighbouring Westminster Bridge just to cross it back once I had reached the opposite shore. Anyhow, the fact was hours had mindlessly passed and the evening had drawn in.

'What time is it?' I asked to the first person I saw, who turned out to be a mother in her mid-thirties strolling with her kid.

'Seven o'clock,' she answered, and went on her way.

I stared at her while she was walking away; I had recognised frustration in her eyes. The gleam is barely perceptible for the great majority but those who had lived it in their bones, the frustration that is frustration, effortlessly recognise it on the others. A young mother, and pretty, strolling with her three year old son on a mild and sunny Summer evening, both smiling… The dream of many, the misfortune of others. I knew it well. I felt pity for her and all those who were still yelling in silence.

I went back to my business. It was seven o'clock, in front of the Big Ben… Then I noticed I could have checked the time on its gigantic face, what a silly mind was mine! I laughed at the absurd of it and stopped a taxi; the desire to sit down had replaced the one to walk.

'Good afternoon, could you drive me to Trafalgar Square?'

'It's quite close, sir, it is just a five-minute walk straight on following this same road,' he said, extremely sincere for a taxi driver talking to a foreigner.

'Yeah, I know, but I don't feel like walking,' as sincere as him.

'Ok, jump in,' and I jumped in. 'All good?' he asked trying to converse.

'All good.'

And that was all the conversation he managed to have for there was no journey for more. We arrived in a minute and I paid him generously with a tenner. I got out of the black cab and stepped into the square jammed with people, tourists above all. When crossing between the fountains I turned around with my arms wide open, took two steps backwards and then turned around again. I climbed the steps in twos up till the last one, on which I sat down with my elbows resting upon my knees. A deep breath. Yes, all good.

I had gone there to find her, my London girl, *my English rose…* —recalling a song I liked—. But now I was feeling at ease immersed in the intimacy which the unknown crowd had bestowed upon me. To feel alone without being alone… Sometimes that could also be a pleasant sensation. Sitting there in the glory, at the top of my world —atop those steps— I was paying attention to the world I had below: to the nonexistent clouds, the cars moving about further down and the people; their gaits, how much they enjoyed making use of their photographic cameras, the face of relief that tourists showed when sitting down after spending all day standing on their feet, the comings and goings of the pigeons, the happy-go-lucky faces of the children and how, curiously, the strawberry ice cream proclaimed itself sovereign champion all over the square, unseating the classic vanilla and humiliating the almighty chocolate. There was a little kid, about three years old, who was playing with his father. The kid with his brand new bicycle with stabilisers would not cease to cross the imaginary line separating his father from the fountain, a five foot line, and as if this were the finish line of the Tour de France the kid would raise his arms —victorious— after what in his mind had been a long and tough race. He reminded me of Sisyphus in some way and I asked myself whether the ease he had to feel such bliss were not, perhaps, because he knew neither Sisyphus nor many others. The happiness of he who knows nothing he shouldn't know, that's how I defined it. Now, with more Tours than all the cyclists in the world united, the kid had decided to cycle away and his father was running after him, worried his son might get hurt. Most people were going up and down the steps without grief nor glory or were stopping only for a moment to take a picture, but there were others who too sat down on the wide stairway, scattered as only chance knows how to do. I could imagine that scene being projected in the cinema, me sitting there, notebook in hand, unaltered while the others would be screened moving in fast motion, along with the sky which in a few seconds would change its light, from the white of the early afternoon to the apricot-red of dusk.

Reality was happening around me as if it were another world, a world I didn't belong to, a world they had excluded me from. They were pointing at me with their finger, they were calling me loco, frightened to say they were just sketches, blurred strokes of a superior mind. My genius had uprisen against me, the created fiction was surpassing me in power and would put that to the test by judging its creator who, for putting in it so much of himself, had left in its hands the sake of his sanity and life. His characters preferred to focus on matter instead of abstracting themselves, of losing themselves in the psyche. Who could blame them considering where all that had led me to? Life shouts, bites, scratches, strikes, tears, mutilates, pushes its way through by giving death to all those aspiring to outlive their progeny. This way, in millions of years' time, when our world will be no more than dust and our souls floating in space, there will be life in the stars feeding itself on light and warmth. Amorphous beings, black as coal, will tell stories about a supposed mankind that dwelled a supposed world green and blue; and, as if our existence were not a conclusive proof of our passage through the universe, they will talk about us as we once talked about dragons, giants, gods and sorcerers.

'England expects that every man will do his duty,' said a voice that I immediately recognised, just right after I had put an end to my reflections.

'Pardon?' The unexpectedness of her words prevented me from getting the complete message.

'I'm not saying anything,' she said, still standing behind me, and remained silent for a few seconds, the time it took her to sit down and land her hand on my leg, with such a natural and loving way that brought me close to tears. 'He's saying it,' pointing, with a gentle movement of her head, to the statue that culminated the enormous column, 'Horatio Nelson.'

'What?' I asked again.

'Don't you know his history? I guess it's understandable for someone who's not from here, but I thought Spanish people knew about the Battle of Trafalgar.'

'How do you know I'm Spanish?'

'I can tell it by your accent. What did you expect?' She said at seeing my face of surprise. 'Your English is good but not that much, mister.'

'I know, I know, but as you didn't say anything before I pleasantly allowed myself to think you had taken me for one of your people. Anyway, and why is it that Spanish people should know about the Battle of Trafalgar?' Displaying my ignorance in all honesty.

'That's so bad…' And she brought her hand to her face when she realised what a scenario she was dealing with. 'The battle took place just west of Cape Trafalgar!' My face didn't show any signs of comprehension. 'Cádiz, Strait of Gibraltar… do these names ring any bells?'

'Ok, I follow you now, but please don't stop, let me hear more.'

'Ok, but I hope you will pay more attention to me than the one you paid once to your History teacher.' I nodded my head. 'The Battle of Trafalgar was a naval battle that took place on 21st October 1805. Do you remember that painting I showed you last Friday?' I nodded my head. 'Well, that ship in the painting was fighting in the battle.'

'The Temeraire.'

'Yeah, that's the one. It seems there's still hope for you.'

'Miss, please, don't make a fool of me,' Oh my… little jokes.

'Well, so in that battle France and Spain joined their fleets together to fight against the British Royal Navy, which was commanded by this man at the time,' pointing at the statue for a second time, 'Vice Admiral Horatio Nelson. By the way, we won,' this last comment with a patriotic pride in her voice, 'thanks to him and his stratagems.'

'And the phrase?'

'It was a message, encoded with hoisted flags, which Horatio Nelson instructed to his signal officer to send to his fleet right before he died in the battle. It was received by a great cheering amongst the sailors and encouraged them even more. We would have smashed you either way, but that gesture made Horatio a man worth remembering. The detail that makes the difference. He really was a great man, he is very much appreciated and admired here amongst his fellow countrymen.'

'I'm sorry to disagree but I do believe he's already forgotten. He's dead, nobody is looking after his interests, nobody calls him to ask how he's doing. You might pay him homage with this abominable column, there may even be a Nelson Street somewhere in the city. Pizzeria Di Angelo?' With my right hand on my right ear, as though it were a mobile phone. 'Could you deliver a Margherita pizza and a quattro formaggi to 42 Nelson Street? No, nothing else, that's all.'

'That's too sad. That man was the leader of great deeds and had an inspiring life, he fought cunningly and with bravery and his country shows him gratitude. But I know you just said that because you resent your past. You can't deny it after what happened yesterday.'

'I'm not resentful, I'm just feeling a bit… you know… this way.'

'This way? Which way?' She asked, inquisitive about my vague and odd reply. I smiled. I had let her twist my arm again and, for it, I thanked her in secret.

'Well, the truth is that I have experimented a series of complex feelings and emotions derived from thoughts which seem to have risen all of a sudden. I think that altered is the right word and I like being altered, I like it so much that I'm planning to be altered all my life and every year, every day, a little more.'

'So, altered, eh… I'm not sure that's the right word, but don't play hard to get with me, tell me the facts.'

'Altered, *alterado*: reckless, agitated, changed, all at once. Anyway, I see I can't give you the runaround.'

'You see you can't,' and she winked at me. 'Come on, tell me.'

'You were right, yesterday, when you said what you said in the bar. I'm studying Aeronautical Engineering. I'm in my third year and although I do believe the story of my academic disenchantment began a long time ago, I can't tell exactly when, for I have the two first years of university very blurry in my mind. Sincerely, the only thing I can tell you about them is that I passed them clean, without failing any subject.

Everything seemed to be fine but within me, well, that's another story. I was so wretched... Looking for some kind of comfort, I would tell myself that after finishing my studies everything would be different, that then I would have earned the right to be happy. I repeated that to myself a great many times, despite intuiting from the very beginning that that would never be the case, because I really needed to believe it. Anyhow, third year came and I enrolled in university just as I had done in the previous years. However, in the first semester I failed one subject. Me!' Hitting my chest with my thumb. 'Who had never failed anything in life.'

'And what happened next?'

'Nothing. Nothing happened. And with nothing I mean nothing bad happened. Two minutes after I had checked my score, I noticed how beautiful the day was. The sun was shining as it had never done before. Then I realised that my failed exam barely mattered to me, and to the others, even less. The world was still spinning around, people were going to work as they did every day, my mother would cook dinner, the teacher that had marked my exam would keep working on his PhD, on Sunday at 10pm the national TV channel would broadcast the film of the week, buses and trains would keep arriving and going with their usual lack of punctuality. And what to say about airplanes and aviation in general? It became evident to me that I was neither missed nor needed there and that, in fact, it wasn't there where I wanted to be.'

'And then you abandoned your studies?' She asked, as if this would have been my only option.

'No, that truth meant that those two years of university, during which I had exerted myself to exhaustion, had been a mistake. And even though I didn't mind failing that subject, I wasn't ready to admit such a failure. So instead of facing that truth I opted to look the other way and enrol in the second semester as everyone expected. I kept going to most classes and even did my homework, but you can't imagine how difficult it is to solve an engineering problem when you are in such a state. It makes trying to focus a hell on earth. The mid-term exams arrived and in the first one I had —I think it was on Aerodynamics—, half an hour after the exam had begun I had not yet solved any of the problems, not even read the statements. Instead, I had written on one of the pages: If three were two, if two were three, how different would the world be around me?' She withdrew her laughter and I laughed along with her, but as everyone who starts laughing before finishing telling a joke, I had to pull myself together and continue. So I did, with my face reddened, trying to contain myself. 'Wait, I haven't finished yet: If three were two,' she burst into laughter again, 'if two were three…' And I joined her with both hands on my stomach.

The people that were around the steps were looking at us and, just when we thought we had calmed down, we looked at each other and fell back onto it. The cycle repeated countless times; it was long since I had laughed in this uncontrollable manner. When the giggling effect passed, I proceeded with my narration:

'Now I'm laughing, but at that moment I didn't think it was funny. In fact, I didn't sit the other mid-term exams. I would tell you I was feeling out of place, strange, alone, contradicted… But if what you want are facts I will tell you that since that moment I proposed myself to ignore my student side and, although I didn't manage to bury it completely, it did stop being my priority. Besides, my conscience was so restless that I would spend my nights sleepless, sleeping only off and on in the mornings and afternoons when insomnia would allow me. Which made it difficult to balance my own schedule with that of the classes, so I stopped attending most of them. I worked just the minimum to get by and not feel bad for lying to my parents when I was calling them and telling them about the lessons I didn't attend. Yes, every night we would call one another and catch up. One night I wanted to speak sincerely, I told them about my demotivation, that I felt all that was not for me. I don't remember the exact conversation, I remember I didn't express myself properly, that they attributed my lack of willpower to the fact that my last exams didn't go well and encouraged me to persevere, to move forward, that I should keep trying and everything would go well. In short, although they shed some tears with me and told me they understood my situation, they gave me to understand that the only way out was to continue my studies. In their defence, I will say that I didn't make myself clear that I was asking them for help, an alternative to the life I was living. I wanted to make myself understood without calling things by their name, like these people who before killing themselves say, at most, that they are sad as their sole cry for help.'

'Is that what it was, a cry for help?'

'Yes, but don't be afraid,' thinking that she might have misinterpreted me, 'I didn't have any intention to commit suicide nor anything of the sort, I appreciate life too much. I just simply wanted a change. I felt very frustrated after that conversation, I had never felt so misunderstood. I remember that after hanging up I lay down on my bed and stayed lying there the twenty-four hours a day has, till the phone rang again. When I picked it up, they soon let me see how they were going to proceed, they would make as if nothing ever happened, as if I had just only thrown a tantrum, a negligible moment of weakness, and I reacted pretending just like them. I didn't show any signs of it, but in that moment I blamed them for all my afflictions.'

'I see, I can imagine the rest…' as if she wished to move the conversation to something else.

Annoyance was my first reaction to her last words, as if she weren't interested in what I was telling her, which in fact was my life. However, after rethinking it and seeing her face somewhat distraught, I realised she might well have good motives: perhaps it was a mistake from my part to mention the word suicide (sometimes I forgot that not everyone shared my insensibility towards death) or perhaps she was just tired after a long day at work. Both motives were justifiable. I decided to ask her about herself, to see if this way she would cheer up.

'I wouldn't know what to tell you.'

'What did you study?' Willing to pull whichever string needed to be pulled to reawaken the conversation.

'Fine Arts,' a sigh and a half smile, at last she seemed to be willing to open up a wee bit. 'I've never told this to anyone but, even though I don't regret it, I think I went into the world of art for the wrong reasons,' her half smile, far from vanishing after her confession, grew to become a complete one. The curative power of words, I thought.

'I'm curious, which were those wrong reasons?'

'You are going to laugh,' while laughing herself, 'there is only one single reason and it is very very absurd. On the same day the London Eye opened for the first time my father took me, also for the first time, to the National Gallery and I fell in love with the place. The paintings were nice and all that, but where my eyes were was on the high ceilings, the pulchritude, the air one could breathe in there and the people, above all on the people. The true art was to observe others contemplate; even to see them walking on the waxed floor came to me as a most inspiring thing to do…'

Then I stopped listening to focus on her hands. They were like a feminine version of mine, with their long and well-drawn fingers but slightly smaller, much finer, more delicate and, of course, prettier. And, although she was talking with enthusiasm about her Fine Arts studies and American films had taught me the importance women give to being heard when they talk, I interrupted her and took the hands with which she was gesticulating so cheerfully. I told her that her hands looked as though they were sculpted by the selfsame Michelangelo, and when I raised my eyes she looked away and blushed. I thought my well-aimed compliment had hit the nail on the head, but I didn't obtain any reply or any sign of approval whatsoever. I did not even hear the dull sound of the hammer. She simply freed one of her hands, in order to be able to turn her gaze to the square without having to twist her neck, and remained in silence. I had been there three hours warming up the step, observing the cosmopolitan landscape and its people while losing myself in thought, but this gaze, hers, had something special in it, an unusual gleam, a reflection almost blinding. Such was it I would have sworn she had her eyes fixed on the light. I was seduced by the idea and did like her. And we remained seated there, hand in hand without saying a word, fading amongst the photons, now golden now red, of a sunset worthy of our favourite painter William Turner. But nothing lasts forever, the nightfall was nightfalling, and one by one were, the first stars, shyly emerging amongst the electric glow of the streetlight.

She didn't say anything about my compliment, but I like to think that if she didn't it was because she actually never heard it, that she was in awe like I with her hands, absorbed in a feature she had just discovered in me, perhaps a rebel lock of my frizzy hair or the green sparkle which ever and anon my hazel eyes could expel. Who knows.

'Do you like cinema?' She asked, still looking straight ahead.

'Few things I enjoy more.' Straight ahead my gaze too.

'Perfect.'

II

During the fifteen minutes that our walk lasted, she wouldn't tell me where she was taking me. She, dressed in her pretty uniform and I with my vagabond looks: three-four days beard, greasy hair and dirty clothes… I thought it and then said it out loud:

'Lady and the Tramp.'

'You are handsomer than what you think,' listening to that comment was like removing a pebble from my shoe.

She stopped walking, we had arrived.

'Film4 Summer Screen 2014?' I read out loud on the poster.

'Somerset House and its annual cinema festival,' she said, trying to shed some light on my bewilderment.

'Interesting. Which film are we going to see?'

'If I'm honest with you, I don't really know.'

'Perfect,' satisfied with her answer.

'Come with me,' and she headed towards the entrance, jumping the whole queue.

'Excuse me miss, you will have to queue like everyone else,' said the hefty security guard, who suddenly quivered and became shy. 'Oh, my apologies, ma'am, I hadn't recognised you with this uniform and the hair upswept.'

'Better?' She asked, after letting her hair down as if she were in a shampoo ad.

'Better,' we both replied, the guard and me, in unison.

'How silly you both are…' she said with a shy laugh.

This way, without tickets, the doorman opened the fence he had behind him and let us in despite, according to the poster, there being ten minutes for the doors to be opened to the public. What did just happen? I asked myself. I got goosebumps when crossing the wide portico. The house's courtyard was a whole square. The imposing façades wore a very particular grey-white-beige tone. On the other hand, the floor… Suffice it to say, when I saw it I imagined, or remembered —I'm not sure—, a film close-up in which there was, rolling on its cobblestones, one of the wheels of those horse drawn carriages of auld lang syne. If it weren't for the big screen and the rest of the cinema equipment, a man could easily be fooled into thinking he had travelled back in time. I was in awe, and I would have walked about shyly if it hadn't been for her, who was now walking with determination towards where seemed to be her favourite spot, right in front of the film projector.

'Are we not going to be too far away?'

'We will see properly, don't worry. Besides, do you see any chairs around? At least here we will be able to lean our backs on the fence,' pointing to the construction fences that were surrounding and protecting the projector.

We sat down. Night was not completely black yet, so I kept turning my head from one side to the other trying to gather every detail of that magical place. London style I would have called it, but in order to remedy my ignorance I decided to ask the expert:

'What is this architectural style called?'

'Neoclassical Architecture, eighteenth century. Pretty, right?'

'If it weren't for the cinema equipment it would look as if we were in a Dickens novel.'

'Have you read Dickens?' She asked with interest, surely willing to engage in a serious literary debate.

'I saw the 1948 film of *Oliver Twist* a year ago. Isn't that enough?'

The ten minutes had passed and our laughs, always proportioned to the absurdity of our most recent exchange of words, escorted the first spectators to their seats —scattered mats on the floor—. The square didn't take long to fill up.

Suddenly, the façades around lit up with a velvety red and the first images appeared on the screen. All the world in silence. The night was black. Let the show begin!

In my first year at university, my Communications teacher said that the first thing a speaker should do is to catch the attention of his audience, and that movie, which turned out to be a recent Irish movie titled *Calvary*, achieved it with the very opening line. The film narrated a week in the life of a parish priest, from a remote town in Ireland, who had to deal with his troublesome parishioners, many of whom felt a not too concealed apathy towards him. It wasn't the greatest film of my life, but it was indeed the best one I had seen that year and, why not say it, one whose watching came across as most opportune. Among other things, it spoke about the hypocrisy and falsehood of people, as well as about the torment that these suffer within themselves. The film was right in that point, everyone has their own handicap, but I wasn't convinced with the way the film treated forgiveness, too exhibitionist for my taste; even so I did appreciate this being one of its main subjects. Besides, I took the appearance of the redhead actress Kelly Reilly as a wink towards me. She wasn't the woman of my dreams but she was equally beautiful. And what can I say about the green plains of the Irish landscape? They made me feel like taking hold of a staff, putting on a hat, and beginning to walk.

When the movie ended, we clapped together with the rest of the spectators and were asked to leave as soon as the credits also came to an end. I was expecting her to talk with some manager so we could linger a little longer in there, but she just followed the congregation towards the exit without saying a thing.

Already in the street, a hundred metres away from Somerset House and the horde hanging out outside, I asked her about what had happened there at the entrance the moment we went in, to which she replied:

'One is entitled to one's own secrets.'

Thereupon we talked about the film we had just watched. I was pleased to see us agreeing in many aspects regarding its aesthetics and ideology. We kept on talking about movies, from *Citizen Kane* to *Harry Potter* passing through *Full Metal Jacket*, *Forrest Gump* and *The Lion King* among others. At some point I mentioned that I would like to be part of that community writing scripts, and she then confessed to me her deepest yearning was to become an actress.

'And why don't you give it a try?'

'I've never taken it seriously. I've taken a few acting lessons and even played Juliet in an amateur production. But I didn't like the profession itself. I liked the idea of seeing myself on the stage interpreting my role, but to learn the text by heart and repeat it until extreme abhorrence seemed tiring. To improvise, on the contrary… There lay the magic. Do you want to improvise a dialogue?'

'But in verse, as in Edmond Rostand's play,' I said, to palliate the bad impression I had caused with my historic lacunas, '*Cyrano de Bergerac.*'

'Perfect!'

'I was being ironic, my lady, perhaps on another occasion.'

'You wicked man, I was so excited to put my acting skills into practice…'

Subsequently, night gobbled us down.

With drunken gaits, among labyrinthine streets, we were choosing our bearings thoughtlessly at every junction; talking about everything and nothing, leaving the everything to the brief silences which, cowardly, we kept interrupting with clumsy words and lucid deliriums. And it filled up, thus, the air, with unspeakable confessions proper to sleepless minds. The atmosphere was intoxicating, she was so pretty and so willing to love me…

'I have to say you are the person I love the most in this world, but I'll be frank with you and say, as well, that I love you and hate you in equal measure,' I said without being too aware of what I was saying. She didn't say anything back and I kept on spitting words, as if my mouth had a life of its own, 'Tonight is a sad night.'

'Why are you telling me this now that we were having so much fun?'

'I don't know, but when I feel that I should be happy I get even sadder.'

'What are you trying to tell me?'

'I'm sorry, I was just drifting away, don't listen to me. Words… they don't really have to speak the truth, let alone have a reason to exist. Don't you think?' At that moment I firmly believed my statement.

'Nevertheless, to disregard their value, even them being only what they are, a stain of ink on paper or a sigh in the air, to disregard their value would be as being blessed with the gift of defecating,' coming out of her mouth not a single word sounded grotesque, 'gold coins and even then flush the toilet.'

'That's why the dog that does not bark pulls the chain!' I wittily said when I remembered one of the sentences with no sense from her white notebook.

'Oh, my god, you are right! The dog doesn't bark because it is indifferent to words, which in this case are its barks, and that's why it pulls the chain.'

Thereon, the conversation took another hue. The atmosphere was intoxicating, she was so pretty, and so willing to love me…

But what I thought to be thoughtlessness was in reality her will; I realised it when we suddenly stopped and she asked me if I wanted to go up to her apartment. Obviously, I agreed to it.

III

When the door opened, I found an empty flat with some cardboard boxes scattered around. Before I had time to say anything she explained herself:

'It's just that I'm moving in at the moment and still have to bring my furniture from my old house. This sofa you see is the only piece of furniture I have now at home.'

I sat down on it, on the left-hand side.

'At least it's comfortable,' it truly was.

She laid down looking at the ceiling, leaning her head upon my right leg. We were both exhausted from the walking and the so very late night. I began to caress her hair.

'What do you write in that black notebook you're always carrying?' it occurred to her to ask.

'I thought you would never ask me.'

'I thought it wouldn't be necessary to ask.'

'*Touché*,' and I began to talk with the clairvoyance long days like this leave behind. 'Throughout these last few months I've written many paragraphs, each disjointed from the rest, some even unfinished. The truth is that their purpose has never bothered me. Besides, I like the disorder on its pages, some packed with words written in all directions; others with only one sentence I push myself to remember. I can open the notebook and write at random on any page, next to a heartfelt confession or under a short story still pending conclusion. Everything is invention, but I'm real, and that bridge that joins what is with what is not turned out to be more solid than brittle, you know? I didn't notice that every time I crossed it something else was moving along, something veracious would crawl into the imaginary, some illusion into reality. I'm not talking about mixing up reality with fiction, but merging both worlds… As if… As if… As if myself being deprived of sleep, I were fated to nevermore wake up.'

I stopped talking, now it was she who was staring at me, with her eyes wide open, asking herself, I thought, whether I was not crazy. And I was, I was speaking up my most intimate thoughts. It might have just been pure foolishness, but at that moment I was worried; she had previously received my demons with benevolence and comprehension but, who can assure us that whoever has killed a dragon can survive the fury of another? She finally articulated some words and cleared things up:

'You were right, altered is the word,' alluding to one of the many unfortunate comments I spoke before the night fell. 'Read me something.'

She gently rolled and bent into fetal position and I, not playing hard to get, leafed through the pages looking to find a decent piece of writing. I found one and slowly read it while caressing her hair:

To what end do we work if at night our dream's not pleasant?
To what end do we love if we are not to be requited?
To what end do we run if there's nothing to flee?
No, I'm not talking about lost causes,
I'm talking about those who go beyond,
that work without demanding in exchange any bonus,
that love for the sake of loving
and run just to run.

'Very nice,' she said, nearly purring. 'Read me more,' nearly asleep.

This time I read her a tale I wrote one night right after having had a few beers in a pub:

They meet in the pub, he wants to ask her out, but when she leaves he only manages to say goodbye. He laments it deeply. He picks up his jacket and says bye to the waiter he's been talking to all night. At the doorstep, when he steps out to leave, she hurriedly steps back in. He goes out and waits for her to go out. Were he to live that same situation again, he would certainly ask her out, he had said to himself barely a minute ago. She goes out through the door and a second time bids him farewell; he doesn't say goodbye, instead he asks her whether she would be interested in going to the cinema sometime next week. She accepts and he gives her his number. He happily goes to bed, it takes him a few hours to fall asleep. Days go by, weeks go by, but she doesn't call. Were he to live again, he would ask her not to leave…

I remember perfectly the moment I conceived that text, and what's curious about it is that I wrote it just like that, in the heat of that same night, before she decided to honour my words and resolved not to call me. Much before I felt relieved for not having received any call.

I came back to the present and noticed she was placidly sleeping. I wanted to lay down and cuddle her, but also feared waking her and ruining that dream which, judging by her face, was one of those for which it was well worth delaying the alarm clock. I was comfortable but not really sleepy, so I kept reading the fragments and gibberish of my notebook.

We shouldn't mistake the search of recognition with the will to please the others, that would be so big an absurdity as trying to discover stars by sweeping the floor; and even then that's what we do, more often than we like to admit, convinced some day the earth will jolt and we will find ourselves upside down sweeping the clouds of an obscure night, discovering hundreds and hundreds of beams of light at each sweep. But what's sad and true is that stars will always be up there and that we do know it, we know it even before taking hold of the brush and starting to sweep.

I had written this one before my journey, as though I were trying to motivate myself to go and look for the change I needed. I would never have thought I would go that far to find it. How much had happened since then…

Sometimes walls start to bite me and don't stop until they have me all chewed up and swallowed. Do you know that feeling? How they lean? What they weigh? Do you really know that feeling? Do you really know what I'm talking about?
I hope you don't.

Bff… I had no recollection of penning this last quote, but I certainly must have had one of my turbulent nights to write with such pain.

I decided to stop reading and, when I went to place the black notebook just on my left, on top of one of the boxes that were still unpacked, I saw there her white notebook. I knew it wasn't the right thing to do, that if I did it I would be violating her intimacy… But the temptation was too much for me.

When you listen to an enthusiastic youth it is inevitable to feel inferior. His words have a weight your voice would be incapable of lifting up. Besides, his eyes gleam ambition and confidence in himself. His spell is powerful, so much that an old man like me can be fooled into thinking that, in the past, something very important was overlooked or that, with the passage of time, that something has been forgotten.

Afterwards the youth resumes his path and the old man remains there, seated, at the end of his. The old man repeats the youth's words to the T., but this time with his hoarse and rough voice; and now, without the hypnotic vitality of the youth present in them, he realises that everything the youth has is enthusiasm and illusion, that he has nothing, that he is empty and still has a long way left to go.

'Emptiness is emptiness,' repeats the old man to himself, 'and it is only filled up by feeling comfortable in it.'

It seems there was something more in that book than sentences with no sense. When I was done reading I asked myself which kind of creature would be capable of writing that, which kind of circumstances he must have been through. But I did only ask, for I didn't feel strong enough at that moment so as to venture on such reflections. I noticed, however, that the two pages that followed that tale —for want of a better name— had been grotesquely stripped off. I yawned. I leafed through the texts that followed. Quickly, brushing my thumb against the edge of the pages. I seemed to notice two different handwritings, I'm not sure. There was in those pages something more than words. I yawned again, I was intrigued but foresaw my departure to the world of dreams was imminent. I placed her notebook back where it was —resting next to mine on top of that improvised nightstand— and, with my left hand entangled in her hair, slowly sank asleep while repeating to myself, as if a mantra, 'emptiness is emptiness, emptiness is emptiness…'

I dreamed about the thickest blackness; dreamed I was dying again and black was becoming blacker. The old man was right, but I didn't have to remain seated, I had to do like the youth and walk with illusion and enthusiasm, even if it were just to reach the limits of nothingness and touch, with my bare hands, its crystal walls.

IV

She woke me up in the worst possible way: lifting up one of my eyelids with her fingers. At that moment I regretted not having stabbed her while she was sleeping. The intense hatred of the moment, for when she put a steaming mug of coffee in my hand, and kissed me on the cheek, I knew I had done the right thing in letting her live.

'Good morning! I'm sorry for lifting up your eyelid, it came to my mind and I couldn't help it. What a disconcerted face you pulled!'

'I wish I always woke up this way.'

'Don't be corny,' she said along with an amiable punch on my shoulder.

I took a sip of coffee, it felt like glory but was still slightly too hot.

'I'm dying for a shower,' I really needed one.

'The bathroom is at the far end on the right.'

The second sip wasn't that hot anymore, so I downed it in four big gulps. Not knowing where to put the mug, I gave it back to her.

'Give me ten minutes,' I said, ingenuously, for as soon as I went into the shower she came in naked behind me.

We showered together. I won't go into details but let's say it was the merriest shower I had ever taken. Once out she offered to put my clothes in the wash, to which I agreed. I gratefully handed my t-shirt to her but said she didn't need to bother with my jeans. She kissed me and went to put the washing machine on. On her way back she threw me a black shirt that was two sizes bigger than my girth. I tried it on and went worriedly to look at myself in the mirror, but no, it didn't made me look like a clown; to tell the truth it suited me and, besides, was very comfy. I'm not sure, but I think she took it out from a box that she had just opened expressly.

'I love this shirt.'

'It's yours then,' she replied absent-mindedly, while searching for the apartment's keys. 'I found them.'

'Where are we going?'

'I haven't planned anything in particular, let's take a walk and we will figure out something as we go, how does that sound?'

'Perfect, but don't you need to go to work?'

'I called in sick earlier,' and winked at me.

Nice morning scene, but in my head still echoed: emptiness is emptiness, emptiness is emptiness…

'You were great yesterday with the sentence of the dog that does not bark, but remember you still have *Necessity is a duck* pending,' she said trying to start a conversation when we were already out in the street.

'Well, I don't know whether it is or is not a duck, but the necessity I now feel is to pull anchor and drift away,' unwilling to postpone the inevitable any longer.

'Again with your divagations?' Remembering my not too fortunate comments from last night.

'Maybe, but this time I do know what they mean.'

'Explain yourself.'

'Well, the truth is that I don't know what they mean but they have somehow more light,' when realising I didn't understand it as much as I had first expressed. 'You know, I began this journey with California being my first destination in mind, and now I'm in London.'

'California?'

'Yes, and I would have taken my flight had it not been for you,' without going into further details. 'It's not that my family were keeping me sane, grounded in reality, but that they impeded me from dreaming, flying… And in a certain way, this is what you are doing,' I said with the most absolute sincerity and the most friendly tone I could find in my repertoire.

'Me?' She asked surprised.

'Yes, you thaw with your sunny smile…' She smiled. 'Yes, this smile, with it you thaw the path that with so much effort moon and night try to pave for me. But please don't take this the wrong way, I'm not saying it is something bad, I love you, as much or even more than the ones I've left behind; you understand me, and that's why I can't fathom why I'm still feeling this necessity to escape from logic and reason, to seek nonsense and chaos in my life as you do well seek in your sentences.'

'If that's what you think, it means you are not as observant as I thought you were. I don't look for nonsense in my sentences, but quite the opposite…'

'Then, why do you call them "sentences with no sense"?' I said sarcastically, interrupting her.

'I don't know,' shrugging and furrowing her brow in a childish manner, 'I suppose I had to name them somehow,' and humbly laughed before getting serious again. 'Ok. Every moment follows one and precedes another. Everything we say and do has consequences, nothing and no one escapes from this law. Look at the clouds for instance, what sense do you see in that cloud over there that looks like a rabbit or a one-winged dragon?' She paused, just long enough to let me raise my head towards the picturesque sky. 'What sense can it have? None! But the cloud does acquire sense from the very moment in which we lay our eyes on it and talk about it, because that means we were here to see it, that at some point our lives crossed paths. This way, something so anodyne as clouds will become a symbol, a nostalgic photograph that will remind us, in addition to reminding us we should take an umbrella before leaving home, that for an instant, in our dispersed lives, we both saw the same when we looked up to the sky,' and with those words she sculpted her undying face amid the clouds. And I say undying because no longer did rains catch me by surprise.

'Damn! Everything is so confusing...' I said in a dispirited tone while mussing up my hair. 'If we could allow ourselves to stop running, breathe unhurriedly and have time to observe and even comprehend everything that surrounds us before change takes place... If only we could slow down the hectic pace with which our lives move forward... Perhaps thus, by dint of deceleration, we could avoid setting a finish line that fades halfway. Perhaps we could recognise deceit when it appears before us. Perhaps...' chocking with emotion. She really had a genuine talent for making me feel vulnerable.

'Calm down, don't despair. Perhaps stopping to think might not be so good an idea, after all every bit of knowledge that doesn't come directly from one's own experience is an empty bit of knowledge, insipid facts bereft of memory. Perhaps we are not as wrong as we think we are, perhaps the right thing to do is just to run, run fast. Even if that means we might stumble from time to time or be forced, at some point, to turn around and take a detour we missed. Think about it, if all we did were thinking, we would just be that, a thought.'

'Then, what do you think I should do?'

'Let's see if I got it right… you began your journey with the idea of going to California stuck in your mind, you wanted to go there and look for a change.'

'That's right,' more calmed.

'But you missed your flight and now you don't know whether to stay or to follow your path to sunny California.'

'Let's say that's a good way to summarise it,' it was incredible the easiness she had to understand everything; I, on the contrary, in the eyes where a few days ago I thought I had seen all the answers, saw now nothing other than mystery and the capacity for comprehension aforedescribed.

Her instructions were precise:

'Then just take a taxi and go to the airport. Buy a flight to California, home or to any other destination, simply say the first place that comes to mind when the attendant asks you where would you like to go. And when you are called to board the plane, you will simply know, you will know what to do.'

'That's your method for everything, right?'

'Indeed, when in doubt the best you can do is to go straight to the threshold and, once there, you don't need to worry anymore: inevitably you will fall towards one side or the other, as easy as that.'

'Taxi!' I shouted when I saw one driving towards us. 'Don't look at me like that, you've convinced me.'

I liked the idea, so I flagged the first taxi I saw. Just like that, violently, which left her baffled. I opened the taxi's door and asked her to jump in with me, which she fain accepted. We didn't talk much while on the road. To tell the truth we didn't talk at all. Sitting one on each side of the car, we had both our gazes lost behind their respective windows. We crossed the green waters of the Thames across the Tower Bridge and lost it, the river, to find it again ten minutes later in the vicinity of where my frozen vision had taken place; from there one could see the great wheel spinning. The taxi driver was driving slowly, for which I thanked him in silence. Subsequently we turned, of course, to Northumberland Avenue, so I could take one last look at my hotel and at the place that had become, without a doubt, my favourite place in London, Trafalgar Square. Afterwards, we drove through the famous The Mall, crossing St. James Park until reaching Buckingham Palace where we spotted the monument to Queen Victoria topped by its seraphic sculpture of golden flares. Subsequently we went across another park which, according to the sign, was called Green Park. I don't know what she had in her mind, but I wanted to think, reflect about what I was going to do, how I should act with her once at the airport, think where I wanted to go; but to no avail, I couldn't focus, I was back on the move, travelling… How nice that was! I had always told myself my weakest point was geography and orientation, but the truth —then I saw it clearly— was that this had never been the case: "The Sun rises in the east and the polar star signals the north; the capital of Angola is Luanda and of Moldova, Chisinau." It was rather an innate predisposition to get lost, aware I would never be any better than in that place called journey, observing the changing landscape of a train with no stops, from which I could contemplate the most colourful flower of Spring without fearing I would afterwards see it wither. And although at that moment I wasn't well aware of it, I had taken my decision already.

We finally reached the airport.

V

We hadn't said anything to each other during the whole drive and, just after going through the airport's glass façade, I heard her sobbing behind me.

'Are you crying? Really? Now you are crying?' I shouted, angry, before I realised I didn't have any reason to react like that. In my defence I will say I was tense, for I was becoming more and more aware that soon I would have to take a life-changing decision and the immediacy of it was troubling me badly. I had crossed the bridge again and everything was again real, my nerves as well; and with these on edge, I proceeded with a tone that itself tried to be more affable and comprehensive, 'Why?'

'Because…' she stopped for a moment and composed herself just to break down again, 'because now you're here with me and I want to cry over you now that you're real, that I can touch you,' while shaking me, 'that I can kiss you,' kissing me on the lips.

Tears came welling up back to my eyes and I hugged her as I had never hugged anyone before, as I have never done again. While she was weeping on my shoulder, with each sob it was more evident to me that, were she to ask me, I would stay in London. However, her request was, as ever, different from what could be expected.

'Hide me from this moment, hide me from time,' she begged.

Inspired, soon I knew what I had to do. I moved her away with a shove; she nearly fell. She interrupted her sobs and looked at me not knowing what to think. I walked around her in circles, looking at her with fascination.

'Whose are these robes, my lady?' said I, playing my role.

'What the hell are you talking about?' answered she, disoriented and furious at the same time. I admit I went slightly too far with the shove.

'This is a masquerade,' I insisted, 'I'm asking about your attire.'

She was still disconcerted —which didn't surprise me— but when, going out of character, I dedicated a smile and a wink to her, she seemed to understand what was going on and became enthusiastic.

'How is it that thou, artificer of this soirée, dost not recognise thy most beloved Juliet?'

'Truth is I never imagined her in such beautiful attire.'

'This is actually how the author describeth her, thou shouldst recognise me effortlessly.'

'Oh, my lady, I was not referring to thy pompous dress; sincerely, whether thou wearest shoes or walkest barefoot I know not, for now that I have thee before me, my dear, such a beautiful personage, am incapable of looking at anything but thy face.'

'And how is this face thou so highly praisest? Describe it to me, describe it to me as if thy voice were a mirror.'

'Oh, my lady, I shall try to fulfil thy request, but permit me to say 'tis not fair what thou dost ask. Admired by men and envied by women, to me thy beauty is what passion is to the artist, it cannot be expressed solely with words. Like the silence of the warrior after the horror of the battle, like the loneliness of the walker that unwillingly walks alone, look at my face, there thou shalt see thy mark! The wish in my eyes… my lips begging for a kiss…'

'I behold thy face and have to say what I see pleaseth me very much, but even more pleaseth me what I hear. Please, keep talking my dear.'

'Forget my face then, and believe me when I say thy beauty is a passion, a battle… that… a battle…' A flabbiness in my speech that I skilfully managed to overcome. 'Thy beauty is the clouds giving birth to a grey day and the cold announcing the come about of a snow-covered night.'

'So cold and so grey dost thou think me?' Pretending to be upset.

'I do love cold and adore grey, *mi señora*.' Kneeled before her, with her left hand between mine.

'Dost thou truly love me?'

'Thou shall recognise my soul amongst the others,' now up on my feet, holding both her hands, 'isolated at the verge of the abyss, and I beg thee, deny me now thy love if that is thy intention, and I will put an end to my suffering by jumping to the void. But if on the contrary thou lovest me do not say a thing, requite my love and I shall suffer in good faith.' Here is an example of the impossibility we experience when trying to escape from our reality. However, we believed the roles we played, not because our interpretations were good, which they weren't, but because we needed to believe them.

This way, the terminal vanished, and in its place there rose up, grey stone after grey stone, a castle. Noble colours covered the enormous walls of a Georgian ballroom with abundant balconies and French windows. Through these could be seen how the whiteness was precipitating over the meadow's green. And inside, fire in the fireplace; hundreds of people dressed in suits and dresses of the epoch were talking cheerfully and drinking wine aplenty. The air was warm and smoky, oppressive to some extent. The clamour was growing louder. It was a great party; greater than I could bear. A few lute chords imposed themselves on the murmur of the gentlefolk and lightened the mood. Cosier, yet still suffocating, I ran to one of the French windows and tried to open it. I couldn't. Then, looking for a way out, I crossed the room to the main entrance and we both coincided seizing in unison the doorknob. Hid amongst the crowd, I had found a girl who was also hiding. And without knowing her I recognised her, she was she.

People were dancing now to a melancholic melody redolent of John Dowland's galliards. The atmosphere was intoxicating, to the point I was tempted to ask her to dance with me, but we went out as we both had planned from the very beginning. And the air was gelid, liberating! We looked at each other and began to run sinking our feet softly into the snow. Thus, running one after the other, inebriate of freedom and youth, we ended up, not knowing how, rolling our fine robes around sheltered mounds of dried grass.

We had evaded it, I thought, and with the thought there it came, there came the present time along and found us loving each other in the men's room as the lovers of bygone days loved each other secretly in the hay.

VI

'What are you thinking?'

Now we were sitting on a bench in the airport's hall, twenty metres from the airlines stands and twenty metres from the exit. By asking me she pierced the bubble that our five minutes of muteness had built, the muteness two lovers go through when trying to assimilate the idea they might not see each other again.

'I was thinking I once heard a phrase, on a TV show or in a movie, I don't know, that said that the cells in our bodies are continuously dying while others are being born and, in this way, after seven years of cellular death and regeneration, we physically become a different person. And now I was thinking that we are now in 2014, and it was in 2007 when I travelled to London for the first time…'

'Seven years.'

'Yes.'

'I should better bid you farewell and leave you alone. I'm glad I found you,' she said, seriously, without the youthful tone that characterised her voice, as if my presence had soothed a deep sadness of hers. 'I truly am.'

Her eyes shone when she held out her hand. And we bid farewell this way, with a handshake. Neither one last "goodbye", nor one last kiss. One last smile as she stood up. When seeing her smiling for the thousandth time I noticed she had one of the two incisors, the first teeth that emerge when smiling, slightly lower than the other. Far from being a vulgar physical defect, it was a most endearing feature. She was unique. Anyway, there is so much to see in a person, that when looking at one we cannot capture all her totality at once, we ought to see her once, and again, and again, and years can pass until the last freckle is spotted or the last smiley expression comes to light.

'Wonderful years…' I murmured when I saw her walking away and thought about the life I would miss were I to take the plane.

In two seconds the Sun reddened and plummeted, light was seeping in through the glass walls of the terminal, dazzling me. I brought my right hand to my brow as an improvised eyeshade, willing to keep my eyes on her and not to miss a single second of film. But the light was growing brighter, she was barely a shadow… Defying the Sun, I kept looking straight at her with my eyes wide open and, when she had already stepped one foot out and had still one foot in, she turned her head towards me, just for a second, before disappearing completely.

In that instant, against the light, her green and grey eyes darkened notoriously, almost black I saw them in the distance, while her hair, blonde, lit by the flares of the twilight, shone reddish just as if I had dreamed her. Ethereal and silent was our first encounter; volatile, her incendiary apparition in St. James Park. But now, finally, she was part of the real world and I thought, that perhaps, a future dance on a frozen Thames wouldn't be so foolish a thing to hope for. We will see each other again I thought, and stopped thinking.

What a liberating sensation that was, like the one experienced seconds before the teacher goes on to distribute the exam to the class: whatever happens, once it's done, whether it has gone well or badly, you won't have to worry about it any longer. At least not for some time, the amount it takes the teacher to correct it. An oasis of peace, that was the square metre in which I was sitting. And making the most of the occasion, I stocked up on calm before getting up and resuming my path.

I finally stood up, my mind still blank, and bought the flight I was predetermined to buy. I passed, without grief nor glory, through the metal detector and went, unaware of my steps, as if advancing all the time on a moving walkway, to my gate. Once there I sat down again.

People were passing by loaded with souvenirs and last minute gifts, others were taking a seat next to me. There were kids troubling their parents, couples holding hands, women and men talking on the phone having the most curious conversations… Others were simply waiting as I was doing, with their gaze lost in the doings of the rest.

With thirty minutes to take off, they announced through the speakers it was now time to embark. I could feel my heart throbbing in my temples, like when the teacher warns he's going to proceed to collect the exams in five minutes and you are still lost in the first problem. To board or not to board, the decision was imminent. People started to get on board and I, looking for something to hold onto, began to write.

We take to all appearances irrational decisions before the alien eyes that with incredulity observe us, for they don't take into account the hurricane of feelings and emotions that make our heart pound like a maniac. They don't understand that before we even get a chance to choose, this has already bolted towards that which we love. And it was she whom I loved, so I missed the flight during the time it took me to weigh my options. I admit I had some regrets when seeing the aircraft taking off, but a few minutes later I clearly felt that what was pushing me to keep on travelling was reason and not the heart itself, as had been the case in the early beginning, and that this same heart now —I smiled at the thought of it— *was telling me not to be like the man who wanted chicken for dinner.*

There was no turning back.

VII

At some thirty-three thousand feet above sea level and at a 0.83 Mach speed, seated next to the window, as it should be, I was reading and re-reading my last note. I was thinking about how I could have gone on board after writing it. Many are the poets who dedicate all their work to love, there are even people who dedicate all their life to it. First to chase it and then to enjoy it. There was a day in which I was one of them myself, and I don't know precisely at which point I stopped worrying about love, but I can certainly say that it was a long time ago since I last thought of it —whatever 'long time' might mean to someone of my age— as I have done so these days. After what had been lived, I was still light years away from summoning a definition that could please me, but I would dare to say that when experiencing it, love, we are capable of relinquishing our conscience and ignoring our self, of letting our soul be twisted so that others don't feel obliged to even bend a bit: for love we listen to our parents and for love we succumb to the yearning of a woman we've barely met. However, our love, when uncoupled long from our needs, spirals into detachment and in detachment so does in turn, as if in chain reaction, our life uncouple from the dreams we hold. Be it in London foreign land or as it had happened previously at home. It must be a universal of sorts: that above love there will always be us and our incessant search, that we fool around switching priorities at our peril, that although love could fill you up as an entire chicken would, sometimes what you need is a duck.

'Necessity is a duck…' I whispered.

JLC

Printed in Great Britain
by Amazon